Dear Reader,

Welcome to the fourth title in the series of *Great Lakes Romances®*, historical fiction full of love and adventure, set in bygone days on North America's vast inland waters.

Like the other four books in this series, *Charlotte of South Manitou Island* relays the excitement and thrills of a tale skillfully told, but does not contain explicit sex, offensive language, or gratuitous violence.

Along with *Charlotte of South Manitou Island*, a Centennial Edition of a romance novel first published in 1894 is also being released. It's a story you won't want to miss! See the back of the book for details.

We invite you to tell us what you would like most to read about in *Great Lakes Romances®*. For your convenience, we have included a survey form at the back of the book. Please fill it out and send it to us, and be sure to watch for the next books in the series, coming in Spring 1993.

Thank you for being a part of *Great Lakes Romances®!*

Sincerely,
The Publishers

P.S. Author Donna Winters loves to hear from her readers. You can write her at P.O. Box 177, Caledonia, MI 49316.

To two women I greatly admire
Anne Severance and Hilda Stahl
for all you've taught me

Charlotte of South Manitou Island

Donna Winters

Great Lakes Romances®
Bigwater Publishing
Caledonia, Michigan

CHARLOTTE OF SOUTH MANITOU ISLAND

Great Lakes Romances® is a registered trademark of Bigwater Publishing,
P.O. Box 177, Caledonia, MI 49316.

Library of Congress Catalog Card Number 92-70331
ISBN 0-923048-79-0

Edited by Anne Severance
Cover art by Patrick Kelley

Printed in the United States of America

92 93 94 95 96 97 98 / CH / 10 9 8 7 6 5 4 3 2 1

Notes

This novel is a work of fiction. Names, characters, places, and incidents are either the product of the author's imagination or, if real, are used fictitiously.

The keeper's quarters diagram has been included to enhance reader understanding of this novel. Though it reflects a degree of accuracy in its detail, it is not intended to reflect reality. In this story, the families of both the head lightkeeper and his assistant occupy the dwelling.

The name, Trevelyn, sounds like Evelyn.

Acknowledgments

I would like to thank the following people:

Bill Herd, of the National Park Service, Empire, Michigan, for historical information about lightkeeping on South Manitou Island

Bob Saddler and Robert Ruchhoft of the National Park Service, South Manitou Island, for making the keeper's quarters accessible for on-site research

Ken Pott and Owen Cecil of the Michigan Maritime Museum, South Haven, for information on yachts and wooden-hulled steamers

Jay Martin, Great Lakes researcher; and Kathy Bietau, former lighthouse interpreter on South Manitou Island, for consultations and advice

Karen Jania of the Bentley Historical Library, Ann Arbor, for research on the University of Michigan—1898

Hilda Stahl for advice on plot and characters which made possible the completion of this book

Patti Smith for her talented pen and ink rendering of the South Manitou Island lighthouse complex on page eight

Pam Chambers for proofreading on short notice.

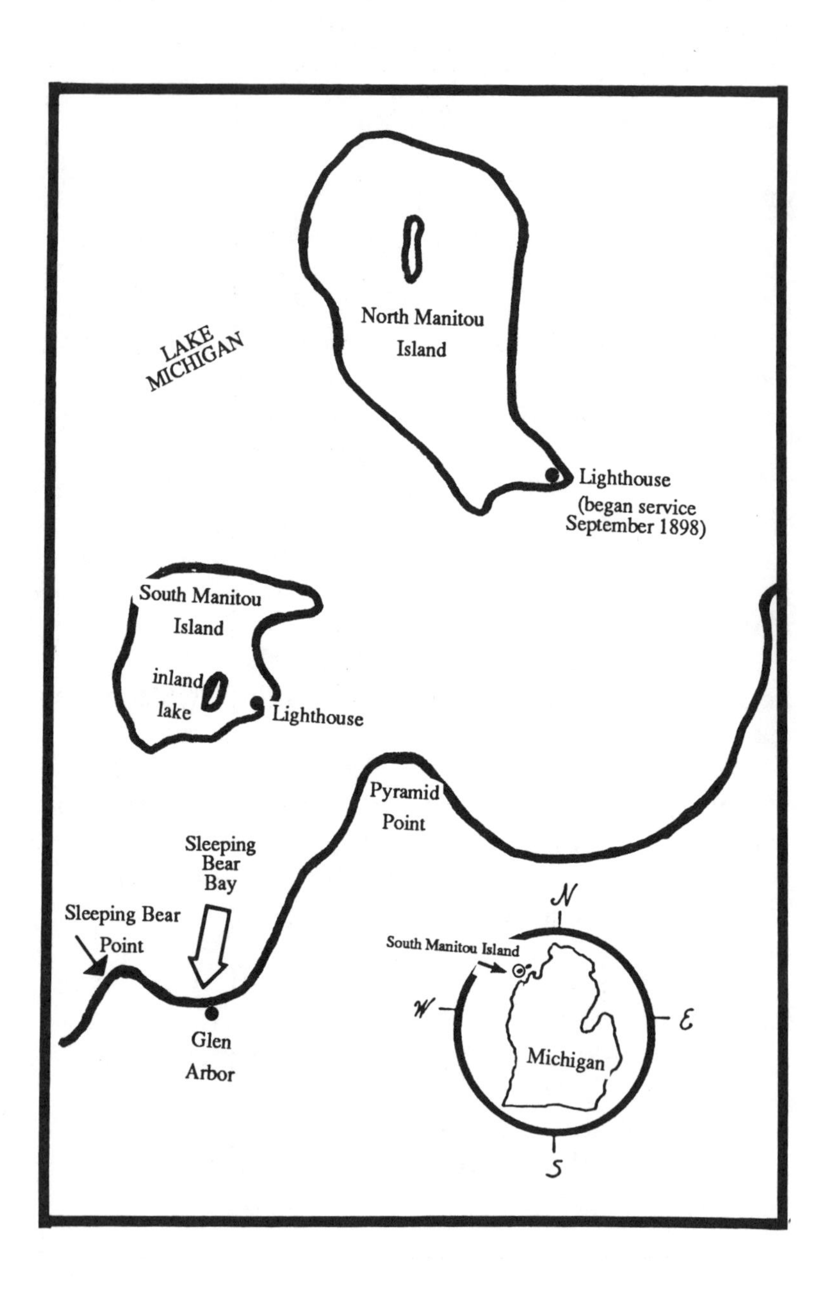
LAKE MICHIGAN
North Manitou Island
Lighthouse (began service September 1898)
South Manitou Island
inland lake
Lighthouse
Pyramid Point
Sleeping Bear Bay
Sleeping Bear Point
Glen Arbor
N
South Manitou Island
W
E
Michigan
S

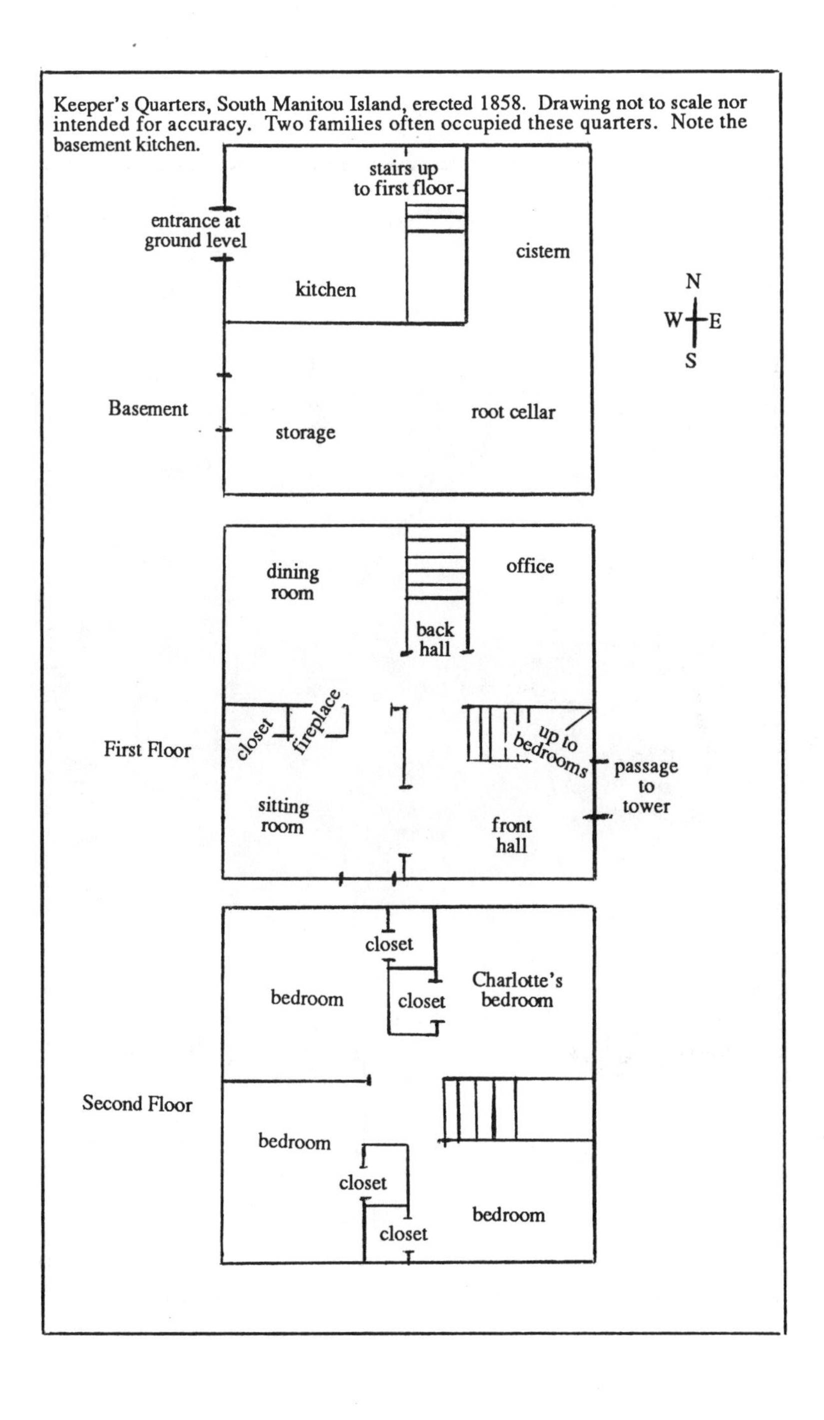

Keeper's Quarters, South Manitou Island, erected 1858. Drawing not to scale nor intended for accuracy. Two families often occupied these quarters. Note the basement kitchen.

SOUTH MANITOU ISLAND LIGHT

CHAPTER 1

South Manitou Island Lighthouse
Keeper's Quarters
Thursday, March 19, 1891

Ten-year-old Charlotte Richards ran up the stairs from the basement kitchen, her waist-length braids flopping against her back. Her father, the assistant lightkeeper, would be proud when she reported that she had again recited her lessons perfectly in school today, and that her teacher had told her she was the best student in the fourth grade class.

At the sound of voices, she stopped outside the office door so as not to interrupt her father's discussion with his boss, the head lightkeeper.

"John, we can't wait another day to go for supplies," Ben Richards insisted. "The beans gave out yesterday. Julia tells me she's only got a half-pound of rice, hardly enough for a kernel apiece in a household of twelve. She served up the last of the pork and beef for dinner last night, and scant portions they were. Her shelves in the root cellar are empty of all but a quart of applesauce and one of strawberries. She's got a bag of cornmeal and a couple dozen eggs left for fryin', but little else." As Charlotte listened from the hallway, she could imagine her father pausing in his conversation with the head lightkeeper to scratch his grizzled beard before continuing.

"To make matters worse, Charlotte told me this mornin' Buttercup has eaten most of her share of the hay you bought from Schroeder last fall."

"The lighthouse tender will surely make her way to us soon," John Trevelyn stated confidently. "Tomorrow morning, I'll hitch up Prancer and take the wagon to Otto Schroeder's and arrange for a few more days' supplies. You can tell your wife her larder will be restocked by noon. I'll bring back some cattle feed, too."

"I've got somethin' else in mind. Nobody expected the *Hayward* to stop by the island yesterday, but since she's cut a path through the ice, and the temperatures are mild, Baase says he's headin' for Glen Arbor tomorrow mornin' at sunrise. I plan to go with him and bring back supplies. With any luck, we'll be back in time for a late supper."

Charlotte's heart sank. Her eleventh birthday tomorrow just wouldn't be the same without Papa.

"I think Baase is pushing his luck on a wooden-hulled boat the size of his," John insisted. "I'd guess there's still a good deal of ice in Sleeping Bear Bay, and spring weather in the Manitou Passage can change in an instant."

"Baase has been out in plenty of spring storms, and so have I," Ben pointed out. "Neither of us is afraid of ice near Glen Arbor. I've set my mind on bringin' back some necessities, and while I'm there, I'll pick up a little somethin' special for my Charlotte's birthday tomorrow."

"You've set your mind on getting off the island," John calmly countered.

Charlotte remembered one day last week when the weather had turned mild, her papa had been irritable, scolding her and her sisters for no good reason. Her mother had explained later that after weeks of isolation, he was anxious to get away from South Manitou for a spell.

"Go if you must," Mr. Trevelyn told her father, "but not on account of our need for supplies. You know as well as I do, we can get by with what's right here on the island."

A silent moment lapsed, then a chair scraped the floor.

Charlotte tiptoed away. She was so disappointed that her father would go away on her birthday, that she no longer wanted to tell him her good news about school.

Her feet dragged on her way upstairs to the bedroom she shared with her two older sisters. She had thought she and her papa shared a very special friendship—more special than he had with her two older sisters. How could he go away on the one day when he was supposed to pay all his attention to her?

She was so upset, it hurt even to think about it. Worse yet, after listening to Mr. Trevelyn, she was worried about her father's safety. Her papa did have very good reasons for leaving the island, or he wouldn't have been so insistent, but she wished with all her heart he would change his mind.

She remained troubled the following morning as she walked the icy path that led to the barn. She had arisen an hour early, as soon as she had heard her folks stir. She had lain awake most of the night anxious over her father's trip, and all the worry had made her hungry for breakfast, but first she must tend to feeding and milking Buttercup. That was the rule—no breakfast until chores were finished.

She pushed the creaky barn door open just wide enough to allow admittance and went straight to work, offering Buttercup the last of her hay. "Sorry girl, but that's all you get for now. The rest of the hay in this barn belongs to Prancer. He's gonna need it to haul home some more for you," she told the brown and white cow, patting her nose before she set her stool and milk pail in place.

To her surprise, Seth Trevelyn reached the barn only a few minutes after she did. So sullen was her mood, she failed to bid "good morning" to the fifteen-year-old at work in the adjacent stall. He slung a feed bag over a chestnut gelding's head, then leaned his arms on the divider between the horse and cow. Charlotte kept her eyes down, on the scuffed toes of his oversized brown leather boots as she sat on the milk stool.

"My, but you sure are quiet. Why so glum? This is supposed to be your happy day, Charlie!" Without even looking, she knew he wore a lopsided grin that showed the overlap of his front teeth.

She ignored the remark about her birthday, and his use of the hated nickname. Her mind was occupied by thoughts of the conversation she had overheard in the back hallway the previous evening as she bent to her task, pressing her head against the cow's flank. With every splash into the pail, her heart sank lower. Just when she thought tears would surely be added to the white liquid, Seth reached down and yanked extra hard on her left braid, then took off.

The pain galvanized her into action. "I'll get you, Seth Trevelyn!" Charlotte flew off her stool, catching up with Seth near the ladder to the loft, shoving hard against his back.

He fell forward, grabbing hold of the ladder, then scrambled up out of Charlotte's reach, laughing as he tossed what remained of the hay down over her. She shook it off and spun away angrily, returning to Buttercup.

Moments later, Seth began cleaning out Prancer's stall, raising a stench as he shoveled manure into the wheelbarrow. He rolled it outdoors, then returned to spread fresh straw on the floor. He finished his work and leaned up against the end post between the two stalls, watching Charlotte. Tears spilled from her tightly shut eyes.

Maybe he had been too hard on the spunky eleven-year-old, he thought. Why was it he just couldn't resist tugging on her long, toffee-colored braids?

He crouched beside her and dabbed her cheek with his handkerchief. She blinked at him, her sad brown eyes lacking the amber highlights that usually made them sparkle. "Sorry, Charli . . . Charlotte. Didn't mean to hurt you."

She took the cloth from him and blew her nose, then looked into his hazel eyes. "You didn't hurt me. Not really." She handed back the damp wad of red printed cotton.

Seth tucked it into his back pocket. "Smile! Things aren't as bad as they seem. They can't be!" he teased.

Charlotte remained somber as she resumed the rhythm of her milking, wishing he would go away.

Carefully, he took one of her braids into his hand and ever so gently tugged on it three times slowly, then three times more in a long-short-long fashion, Morse code for "O.K." It was a lantern signal his father used when out on the lake in dark, rough weather, a way of letting his family know he was coming in safely. When Charlie first arrived on South Manitou, Seth had made a question of it to see if she could repeat the pattern accurately. Usually, she played back the rhythm by tugging on his earlobe. Today, he got no response.

"Want to tell me what's wrong?" Seth asked.

When Charlotte remained silent, he continued. "I bet you've forgotten the words we went over last night for your spelling bee in school today."

"Have not," she answered glumly.

"Then how do you spell jollity?"

"J-o-l-l-i-t-y."

"Snappish."

"S-n-a-p-p-i-s-h."

"Birthday."

"That wasn't one of our words, and you know it! Now go away and leave me alone."

After a moment's contemplation, Seth wandered off.

When Charlotte had stripped Buttercup dry, she set her milk bucket aside and went to put away her stool. By the time she had come back to get the pail, Seth had already carried it to the door where he was waiting for her.

"You still haven't told me what's wrong," he reminded her.

She stepped out into a biting, gusty wind. "Papa's going to Glen Arbor with Mr. Baase this morning. Now he won't be home for my birthday," she said downheartedly.

Seth paused to pull his stocking cap over his thick, sandy hair. "Maybe your papa won't be here, but I will, and so will Nat, and Aurora and Bridget and Dorin and Eli and your mother and my folks." He named his seventeen-year-old brother and all of Charlotte's siblings, from her twelve- and thirteen-year-old sisters down to her two- and one-year-old brothers.

"I know," Charlotte responded unenthusiastically.

Seth held open the ground level door at the back of the two-story yellow brick house, allowing entry into the warm basement kitchen. The aroma of corn dodger and coffee greeted Charlotte. She stamped the snow off her feet on the sisal mat, hung her coat on a peg and pulled off her boots, then washed her hands at the pump in the sink to the left of the door. The huge iron cook stove behind her warmed her back. She held her hands over it a few moments, then followed Seth up the steps to the first floor dining room where her mother was already serving breakfast to her father.

They seemed a perfect pair, Charlotte often thought, both plump, both with kind round faces and dark hair—her mother's pulled loosely away from her face and wound into a tidy knot atop her head, her father's a bit unruly, covering his ears and brushing his collar in the back.

"Good morning, Charlotte. Happy birthday!" Her father greeted her as she took her place opposite Seth at the oblong oak table and tucked the point of her napkin inside the neckline of her gray flannel dress.

"Good morning," she muttered.

Her mother poured two glasses of milk, and passed the platter of corn cakes to her and Seth. While he hungrily consumed a syrup-drenched patty, she picked at hers, despite her growling stomach. To her, the cornmeal was a distasteful reminder that the supply of flour had run out.

Her father stabbed another patty from the platter, dropped it onto his plate with the help of his fingers, then drenched it in syrup. "I'm sorry I won't be home for your birthday, Charlotte. I'm going to Glen Arbor."

Charlotte put down her fork. "Please don't go, Papa. Not on my birthday!" she pleaded.

He chewed and swallowed quickly. "But I'm going to bring you something special."

"I don't want something from Glen Arbor. I want you here, all to myself," she brooded.

Hastily, he took another large bite, washing it down with a gulp of coffee. "I know I promised we'd spend time together, just you and me, but plans have changed. I'll try to be back for supper at the usual hour, but if I'm not, you eat without me."

"You could go a different day," Charlotte argued.

He set his fork down and looked pointedly at her. "That's enough, young lady. You'll be in school most of the day. Speakin' of which, you tell your sisters for me they're to start in on their arithmetic lessons the minute they get home. No waitin' till Sunday night to do Friday's assignments. At least I don't have to worry 'bout you. Your cipherin' is always done by Saturday." He shoved back from the table. "Now I've gotta get on over to the dock. Wanna come with me, Charlotte? There's time before school starts."

Charlotte hung her head, pouting.

He paused beside her, his hand on her shoulder. "Now don't be like that. Come and see me off."

His attempt to placate her acted like a match near a kerosene-soaked wick. She jerked her shoulder away and jumped up. "I won't go! Besides, I don't care if I never see you again!" She ran out of the dining room and up the stairs, nearly colliding with her sisters on their way down to breakfast.

She slammed the bedroom door and flopped onto her

bed, burying her face in her pillow. Tears dampened her pillow case as she tried to figure out whether she was feeling sorry for what she had said, or angry that her father was going away. For half an hour she sobbed quietly. Steeped in self-pity, she put on a shawl and climbed up in the light tower to watch for Baase's boat leaving the harbor.

Today, the hundred and twenty-some winding stairs to the balcony seemed endless. She opened the door slowly and peeked out at the harbor, with its melting mounds of snow along the horseshoe-curved shoreline, and the harbor waters—still thick and white with ice at the shore; thin, dark, and marred by the path of the *Hayward* farther out; and completely melted in the distance. There, in the open water beyond the dock, was Baase's boat. At the stern stood her father. The instant he waved to her, the anger within sparked anew, and she jumped back inside the tower, out of sight, her hands clenched at her sides. "I won't wave to you, Papa. I won't!"

Despite the small birthday celebration for her at school, Charlotte remained troubled over her father's departure. In addition, guilt had set in over her behavior toward him. The day seemed to drag. Her desk mate and good friend, Meta Schroeder, couldn't seem to understand why she was unhappy on her birthday.

When school let out, Charlotte went directly to the watch room, about two-thirds of the way up the one-hundred-foot light tower. Mr. Trevelyn was already in the lamp room at the very top. Dusk was closing in, and she could tell from the acrid scent of kerosene that he had just filled and lit the Third Order lamp. Charlotte searched the passage waters with Mr. Trevelyn's binoculars in the slim hope that her father might make it home earlier than expected. She was eager to apologize, to put the misery of this day behind her. She imagined running to his outstretched arms for a huge hug. But there was no evidence of traffic on the lake. Dejectedly, she descended the iron stairs.

The moment she came through the passageway connecting the lighthouse to the keeper's quarters, she could smell her mother's garden herbs of parsley and thyme, and the vegetables and beef of her mother's stew simmering—Charlotte's favorite. She knew then that Mr. Trevelyn had been to Schroeders for supplies as he had promised.

When her mother and sisters and the Trevelyns gathered around the table, she felt an emptiness in her heart at the sight of the vacant chair normally occupied by her father. Though the stew was as delicious as usual, rich with large cubes of tender meat and chunks of potato and carrot, Charlotte found little joy in the occasion, even when her mother brought her chocolate birthday cake to the table. The first piece she cut was a generous helping set aside for her father.

After the table had been cleared, several presents appeared in front of her, small tissue-wrapped items. She opened them slowly and tried desperately to sound enthusiastic with her thanks. Since no one had been able to leave the island for weeks, the gifts were either fashioned by hand, or previously owned. From Seth came a tiny, slightly dog-eared volume of *Peter Piper's Practical Principles of Plain and Perfect Pronunciation.* It was the only book she received, and it had obviously seen many readings in his childhood. But she cherished it because she loved books more than anything, and in the months since she had come to live with the Trevelyns, he had been clever enough to figure out what would please her most.

By Charlotte's bedtime, the weather had turned colder and the wind had kicked up, rattling the windows in the second-floor bedroom she shared with her two older sisters, but her father had not yet returned. Twice during the night she got up to look for a sign of the Baase boat. No vessel could be seen in the white beam issuing from the tower.

Daylight gradually followed the seemingly endless night. At half-past noon, Charlotte checked the tower window for the tenth time that day, but found no boats nearing South Manitou. "Papa, *please* come home," she begged, knowing her heart would remain heavy until she could be with him.

Half an hour later when she again climbed the tower, she *did* see a boat entering the harbor—not Baase's mail boat, but a larger one—the lighthouse tender. She ran down the spiral stairs as fast as her feet would carry her to spread the news of the inspector's arrival.

Charlotte changed into the clean pinafore her mother gave her, worrying all the while that her father might be in trouble when the inspector learned he had gone on leave and was way past due to return. She helped her mother don a clean, white, stiffly starched apron, then stuffed the soiled one into the hamper for her. While Aurora and Bridget each took one of their younger brothers and changed them into clean gowns, Charlotte went from room to room with her mother, straightening, picking up, putting out of sight any article that could be hidden away in a drawer or cupboard. They dared not stow clutter in the closets, for the inspector would be certain to look inside each one.

Neither were bedrooms off limits. Demerits would be

issued for smudges on plaster walls or for unmade beds, as well as for fingerprints on the Fresnel lens in the light tower. Too soon, Inspector Gordon came through the gate of the white fence that encircled the light tower, keeper's quarters, fog signal building, oil house, privy, and barn.

Charlotte had expected him to go straight up to the lantern room, but he entered the keeper's quarters first. The moment she saw the grim look on his face, and that of Mr. Trevelyn's, she knew something was terribly wrong. Inspector Gordon met with her mother and Mr. Trevelyn in the office for a long, long time, while Mrs. Trevelyn kept an eye on the children in the front sitting room, making certain her own two boys were dressed neatly, and that Aurora and Bridget and their young charges, Dorin and Eli, maintained some semblance of decorum.

Charlotte kept slipping away to the rear of the house to listen outside the closed office door, but each time Mrs. Trevelyn would call her back to the sitting room. Finally, she asked Charlotte to read to everyone from *Peter Piper's Practical Principles of Plain and Perfect Pronunciation.*

She read the book all the way through, then started over again. The second time she came to "Walter Waddle won a walking wager," the office door opened.

Inspector Gordon, Mr. Trevelyn, and Charlotte's mother entered the sitting room, and Mrs. Trevelyn took her own sons and Charlotte's little brothers upstairs. Her mother began to weep softly.

Alarmed, Charlotte and her sisters hurried to their mother's side. "Mama, why are you crying?" Charlotte asked.

Her mother wept harder, pressing her damp handkerchief to her face. Evidently unable to speak, she looked to

Inspector Gordon. He cleared his throat and shifted his weight from one foot to the other. Tucking his hat beneath his arm, he raked his fingers through his thinning gray hair, then jammed his hand into his pocket and jingled his coins. "The ice . . . Baase couldn't get through. Your pa tried walking across it. He . . . he didn't make it. I'm sorry, girls. He's . . . dead."

Charlotte stepped back from her mother and faced the inspector squarely. "Papa isn't dead. He can't be!" she countered.

"Charlotte!" her mother scolded through her tears.

Charlotte put her hands on her hips, speaking boldly. "Papa's not dead. I just know it. He's *not* dead!"

Her mother blew her nose and stifled her sobs. "Charlotte, go to your room this instant!"

"I won't go! Not until Inspector Gordon tells the truth! Not until he says Papa's coming back!"

"Inspector Gordon *has* told the truth," Charlotte's mother insisted. "Papa has come back to us . . . in a coffin."

Charlotte's eyes blurred, her mind spun, her voice cried out, emitting an hysterical scream. She bolted out of the room.

CHAPTER 2

March 1892

Charlotte pulled the quilt off her bed and wrapped it around her shoulders to ward off the damp chill in the upstairs bedroom, then leaned against the headboard to stare out the window at the white tower that was growing gray with the onset of dusk. She pondered how her day had turned into a disaster.

The scolding she had received in school for failing to recite her lessons had been bad enough, but then she had come home and promptly gotten into an argument with her mother. What a horrible way to end a Friday!

She just didn't care about her schoolwork anymore, and she never had been any good at controlling her temper. One year after her father's death, all she could think about was how guilty she felt for having told him she never wanted to see him again. She wanted to tell him she hadn't really meant it. If only she hadn't said those words, maybe he would still be alive!

How desperately Charlotte wanted to return to the time soon after they had arrived on South Manitou when she had reached the "magic age," as her father had called it, the point in a child's life when she was old enough to understand how to properly clean the fragile lens prisms, but still young enough to fit her slender fingers in the narrow spaces that separated them one from another.

The first summer on South Manitou, she remembered fondly, had been a special time between them. With school in recess, she had been free to help for hours on end in the tower room.

He had loved to spin stories about lightkeeping, and no matter how many times he repeated them, she never tired of his spellbinding voice. He could embellish the same old tale in any number of ways, sometimes asking her to choose what happened next, and with her help they would make up a new tale. Between them, they must have had a dozen versions of the story about St. Martin Island in Green Bay, where according to legend, the keeper still searched for his missing children by a green lantern light that sometimes appeared mysteriously on its southwest shore.

Lamp and lens cleaning always passed quickly in those days when Charlotte didn't have to share her father's attention with anyone else in the family. He told her she was the best of his three girls at cleaning glass.

"Your sisters were good at it," he'd say, "but not like you, Charlotte. You have a keen eye for findin' fingerprints."

Turning his pocket inside out, he would reward her efforts with a penny, if he had one. Many days, his pockets were empty, and her reward was a pat on the shoulder and a kiss on the forehead.

Now her mother was assistant keeper and spent as much time cleaning the lens and lantern and standing watch as her father had. But not once during the past year had Charlotte gone into the lamp room. Her mother and Mr. Trevelyn had both invited her on a number of occasions to help with the cleaning chores, but she had resolutely stayed clear until Mr. Trevelyn had put out the tower light for the winter in December. Now spring had come again. Tomorrow, Mr. Trevelyn would light the lamp for the first time this season. Charlotte's mother had told her she was to help him with the work in the lamp room in the morning, and the very thought of it had put her into a tantrum.

Darkness of night now shrouded the tower. She reached for the rag doll leaning against the footboard and laid it against her pillow, rearranged the quilt over her bed, and settled beneath it into the cozy, soft down mattress. But even the comforting scent of the rosewater she had put on her dolly last night could not soothe her soul. Somehow she would get through this night of loneliness and sad remembrances. Somehow, too, she would get over the anger that didn't seem to go away.

By Saturday morning, like the thick gray clouds that had settled over the island, a heaviness had settled in Charlotte's stomach. As she hurried to the barn to feed and milk Buttercup, she could think of nothing but how horribly she had behaved on the last day she had seen her papa.

After chores, she managed to keep to herself, avoiding conversation during breakfast that might draw her into an argument. Quickly finishing the meal, she carried the last of the dirty breakfast dishes down to the kitchen where Aurora was washing up. Bridget was feeding Eli in his high chair, and keeping an eye on Dorin, who tended to race in and out of the room at will. Her mother stood at the baker's cabinet, measuring out spices for molasses cookies. Charlotte picked up a dish towel and began drying the plates.

Her mother closed the tiny drawers holding ginger, cinnamon, nutmeg, and cloves, and turned to Charlotte. "I'd like you to go up to the tower room now. Mr. Trevelyn needs your help."

Charlotte cringed inwardly. She had hoped she had heard the last of that subject yesterday afternoon. She put away the plate she had just dried and picked up another. "I'll go as soon as I finish helping Aurora," she answered sullenly.

"Like I said, Mr. Trevelyn needs your help *now*. Bridget will dry dishes when she's finished feeding Eli."

Bridget moaned.

Charlotte wiped the plate she was holding, put it on the shelf, and picked up a handful of silverware from the pan of rinse water. "I'd rather help Aurora first. Mr. Trevelyn won't mind."

"But I will," her mother said adamantly. "Don't be disobedient, Charlotte. You know what that gets you." She dusted her hands on her apron and reached for the corn broom leaning against her cabinet. "You're not too old for me to take this to your backside."

The more insistent her mother's tone, the more determined was Charlotte to stay clear of the light tower. She couldn't face going into the place which had become the sacred tomb of so many cherished memories.

Her mother took one step toward her and tapped the floor with the broom. "Go on. Do as I say."

Anger sizzled inside Charlotte, threatening to flare up. She dropped the silverware onto the kitchen table with a clank, threw the towel down on top, and ran upstairs, grabbing her coat from the peg as she left. From the back hallway, where she stopped to pull on the faded and worn red woolen tog, she could see that Mrs. Trevelyn was in the office at her husband's desk bringing up to date the list of supplies that had been depleted at the light station. Charlotte was thankful the woman was too preoccupied to pay her much notice.

Charlotte hurried to the front sitting room and snatched *David Copperfield* from the portable lighthouse library, tucked the book beneath her coat and rushed out through the passageway to the lighthouse. When she reached the tower, rather than climbing the stairs to the lamp room, she ran outside and circled around to the back, heading for the barn.

Seth and Nat would already be there cleaning out stalls, their usual morning task. Quietly, Charlotte snuck in the small side door, being careful not to let the squeaky hinge give her away. She waited silently until both the boys had gone out the big door at the end of the barn, then climbed the ladder to the loft. Quickly, she built a mound of hay by the window where the dim light of the overcast day was just bright enough to read by, then scrunched down so Seth wouldn't notice her when he came up to pitch off a fresh supply of hay.

She tried to read, but was too distracted by Nat's and Seth's voices and movements to concentrate. Within moments, it seemed, Seth had climbed to the loft. His conversation with Nat seemed exceptionally loud.

"I wonder if Charlie will help in the lighthouse this year," Seth seemed to shout.

Nat's answer, from the barn floor, was nearly as audible. "I doubt it. Anyone who even mentions she ought to go up to the tower room could be in for a real fit. Seems strange to me that since her pa's been gone, she's acted mean around here, rather than nice, like her sisters."

The comment about Charlotte's older sisters really rankled. For most of her life, she had idolized them and tried to win their approval. For several months now, she had earned nothing but their criticism—well-deserved criticism at that, she realized.

Seth pitched down another forkful of hay. "She puts on a show, all right. I heard her mama tell Pa just yesterday that Charlie refuses to do her school lessons, and she's been sent to the corner at least once a week by her teacher. Mrs. Richards said she'd give Charlie one more chance to get over whatever it is that's making her ornery, and if she doesn't, she's gonna take her on the first boat to the mainland this spring. Maybe somebody over there can get some work out of her. Charlie's sure not much use around here if she won't go up in the lighthouse, but her ma could make use of the money from her labor, with four others to raise."

"I'd hate to see little spitfire wind up in Glen Arbor with Mr. Hardacker," Nat conjectured. "He'd probably hire her right off. I hear he's a mighty tough boss. Cracks his whip over his people from sun up to sun down, except for the few minutes he gives them to eat their gruel for lunch. Makes life at the lighthouse seem like a vacation, from what I've been told."

"Charlie will wish she were back here, all right," Seth concluded.

"Guess I'm done here. I'm going in now," Nat said, slamming the creaky door as he left.

Charlotte could hear Seth moving closer to her hiding

place in the hay. She held her breath until she felt three painful pricks on her bottom side. She jumped up, her eyes flashing fire. "How *dare* you poke me with that fork, Seth Trevelyn!"

He laughed. "Well, what do you know, it's little Charlie!"

She raised her book, intending to throw it at him, but thought better of it, lest she damage light service property. "Don't call me Charlie!"

"Charlotte, then. What are you doing out here? You're supposed to be up in the light tower helping Papa. Bad things happen to little girls who don't mind their mother."

"I heard what you said about Mama sending me away to work for some mean man in Glen Arbor. Maybe I *have* been naughty, but she'd never do that."

Seth's left eye narrowed to a slit, while his right brow moved upward. "I wouldn't be at all sure about that, if I were you, young lady," he warned. "This past year you've had a grouch on more times than a body could count. Not only that, you've been surly, rude, impudent, sassy, and uncivil—sometimes all in the same day."

"Have not!"

"See? There you go, talking back. You know I'm telling the truth, you just don't want to own up to it."

Seth's words stung, but she was determined to put up a strong front. "I don't have to listen to you anymore!" She bolted past, heading for the ladder from the loft, but he caught her by the collar and pulled her back, swinging her around to face him.

"You're not leaving this loft until you've heard me out, so you might as well make yourself comfortable." He pushed her gently down on the hay. "You can't fool me,

Charlotte. I know why you've been ornery as a bull in a pen this past year. It's because of what you said to your pa the last time you saw him."

Her chin on her chest, she mumbled, "Is not."

"Sure it is." He crouched down beside her. "I remember sitting across from you at the breakfast table when you told him you didn't care if you never saw him again. Then, when it came true, you blamed yourself because he died." His tone was empathetic. "That's it, isn't it?"

A knife twisted in Charlotte's stomach. How could Seth have figured out her very darkest, innermost secret? She pressed her hands over her ears, shaking her head violently.

"No, no, no!"

Though she squeezed her eyes shut, she couldn't keep the tears from leaking out.

Seth dabbed at them with his handkerchief, then took her hands and held them firmly in his. "It's all right," He spoke softly. "What you said didn't make your father die."

She looked up at him, her face contorted with anguish, and Seth's heart wrenched.

"Did so," she mumbled, sniffing to keep her nose from running. "It's all my fault. Sometimes, I wish I were dead!"

Seth gave her his handkerchief to blow her nose, then drew her into his arms, pressing her head against his heart—a heart that was breaking right along with hers. He could barely speak past the lump that had lodged in his throat. "Oh, no! Don't ever wish that! It wasn't your fault!"

His words seemed to make her weep all the more. He held her until the sobbing began to subside, then set her apart and lifted her chin, looking into her damp face. "Listen, Charlie, what happened, happened. Anger and tears won't change things. It's time to leave the past behind." He brushed her cheek with his thumb. "And it's time to smile again. I sure have missed your smile, Charlie. Could you smile for me right now? Just a little bit?" He pressed his fingers against the corners of her mouth, forcing them upward.

Charlotte felt as though the heavy burden she had been straining under for the past year was beginning to lift. Though she still didn't feel like smiling, she forced herself to do it for the sake of this fellow who had been part brother, part friend, even when she had wanted neither.

Seth could tell even the tiny, tight-lipped smile that lasted but a few seconds had cost Charlotte a great effort. He tried to encourage her with a smile of his own, but he could see that she was still on the brink of tears. Lifting her braid from her shoulder, he tugged out the Morse code pattern for O.K.

A year had passed since he had last played that rhythm on her braid. Though a tear rolled down her cheek, she reached up, pulling on his earlobe. Three long tugs, followed by a long-short-long. Then she threw her arms about his neck and whispered in his ear. "Thanks, Seth, for sticking by me."

The big hug he gave her said more than words ever could have.

She released him, and he took her by the hands, pulling her to her feet. "Come on, Charlie. It's time to go pay Dad a visit in the light tower."

She hesitated. "I can't go up there."

He picked up her book, stuck it in his oversize pocket,

and pulled her toward the ladder. "Sure you can. I'll go with you."

Reluctantly, she went along, descending the ladder, dreading every step that took her out of the barn, across the yard and closer to the one-hundred-foot tower. Seth urged her through the door, then followed her up the iron stairs.

When she reached the trap door just below the lamp room, she froze. "I can't go in there," she said.

Though Seth could hear the dread in her voice, he said firmly, "Yes, you can. You've got to."

In the tower room above them, Mr. Trevelyn must have overheard them, for he spoke warmly. "Come on up, Charlotte. I've got buff cloths and wine spirits and dirty lens prisms all waiting."

She glanced down at Seth.

He gave her a determined look, and whispered, "Go on."

She took the remaining steps slowly, trying to ignore the leaden ball of dread in her stomach, and the ache in her heart. The vinegar-like scent of the cleaning fluid drifted down to her, beckoning her, until at last she emerged in the lamp room, her heart hammering.

Mr. Trevelyn's mouth curved in a broad, easy smile above the bushy gray beard on his chin, helping to quell her anxiety. He handed her a linen apron, light service issue to prevent scratching the glass, and helped her tie it on, folding it over at the waist like her father always had, to keep it from dragging on the floor and tripping her. Although it was still much too generous, the fit wasn't quite as bad as the last time she had worn one. She had grown taller since that long-ago day when her papa had put an extra knot in her apron strings.

Unlike her father, Mr. Trevelyn was tall and thin, with a shock of gray hair spilling onto his forehead, an infinitely patient man. Her papa had been of medium height, and too full of nervous energy to ever stop fussing.

Mr. Trevelyn kept up a patter as they worked. Despite his efforts to involve her in conversation, she could only offer stiff, monosyllabic answers to his questions.

He did not make up interesting tales and ask her to help with the endings. He talked of his duties in the light service, of moving from Wisconsin a few years earlier.

He spoke of his parents, and those of his wife still living in Milwaukee, and the recent news that Grace, his oldest, would soon deliver his first grandchild in that city. Adult talk. Boring talk. She barely listened as she concentrated on the prisms, inspecting each one carefully after cleaning to see that no smudges remained before moving methodically to the next.

After awhile, he changed to a topic that caught her attention. "I know this year's been a rough one for you, Charlotte. Losing Ben has been hard on us all. But there comes a time you've got to get beyond the hurt. There's one thing I know for sure about your daddy. He wouldn't be pleased at all if he thought you were losing out on life because of his accident. If he could talk to you right now, he'd tell you to get on with it. That's why your mother stopped asking, and just plain told you to come up here and help out today. For a while there, I was pretty sure you weren't going to show up, but I'm awful glad you did." He finished wiping a prism and set it carefully back into its proper place. "You know what your mother told me the other day?"

Charlotte kept her silence, wondering if he would

divulge the plan to send her to Glen Arbor to work.

He paused only briefly before answering his own question. "She said despite what's happened, life can be good, if you let it, and she had hoped you'd soon see that for yourself, now that your papa's been gone awhile." He untied his apron.

Relief washed over her. How she wished her mama had talked to her about such things, but she supposed that hadn't been possible with the way she had been acting.

Mr. Trevelyn hung up his apron. "We're done here, Charlotte. Would you like me to untie your apron?"

She fumbled with the knot at the back of her waist, then turned around, letting him help her with the strings that seemed hopelessly tangled. He hung her apron beside his, just like her father always had.

She could feel the moisture beginning to well in her eyes again. "Thank you, Mr. Trevelyn," she managed, before her throat closed in a knot.

She ran out of the lamp room, taking the steps as quickly as she could. Rather than exiting through the passageway into the house, she continued all the way down the stairs to the bottom, running out onto the snowy beach.

There, she stood looking up into the heavens that were beginning to reveal sunshine and brilliant blue between the heavy gray and white patches.

She drew a deep breath of the cool damp air. "Papa, I hope you're listening," she said a bit self-consciously. "I've got something important to tell you."

Charlotte thought about the gray clouds, and the breeze that parted them, revealing an azure canopy and bright sunlight. Now, for the first time since her father's death, it seemed as though sunlight was coming back into her life.

Just like a lighthouse tower lamp is extinguished for the winter, the light inside her had gone out, and like a newly lit incandescent oil vapor flame, she had needed time to adjust before she could return to her full potential.

"Papa, if you're listening, I'm awfully sorry for the way I've acted since . . . you went away." She blinked to keep the tears from blurring her vision of the pretty sky. "I promise you I'm going to smile more, and I'm going to try to behave better." She looked down, kicking the snow, then raised her face to the heavens again. "And one more thing, Papa. I'm going to do better in school, too."

She scooped up a wad of snow, patted it into a ball, and threw it as far as she could, smashing it on the ice several yards away, hoping to destroy with it the temper she had indulged for the past twelve months.

CHAPTER 3

May 1893

"Mama, may I ask you about something?"

Charlotte had been waiting for an opportunity to speak to her mother alone. It seemed ironic, after avoiding the situation for the past year in the event that Seth had been right, that her mother planned to send her to work for Mr. Hardacker in Glen Arbor. It was a subject neither of them had ever spoken of. Evidently, Charlotte had improved enough in her temper and helpfulness at home and her citizenship and grades in school to show her mother that she was worth keeping in the Richards family.

Now, after fourteen months of studying, thinking, and conversations with her papa, Charlotte had discovered a definite direction for her life. It was one that required her mother's advice, and tonight seemed like the time to seek it. Dorin and Eli had finally settled down for the night. Aurora was downstairs at the dining table working on the sewing she had taken in, Bridget had gone for a walk along the moonlit beach, and the Trevelyns—after making certain the lamp was lit and properly adjusted—had decided to visit their good friends, the Schroeders. They had invited Charlotte to join them, knowing of her friendship with Meta, but she had her mind set on this chance to be alone with her mother, who had recently taken up watch of the light from her favorite place, the rocker by the window in her daughters' bedroom.

Julia looked up from her darning, peering with pale blue eyes above the half-glasses she needed for close work. The smile that formed readily put dimples into her ample cheeks. "Certainly, Charlotte. Come sit on your bed and tell me what's on your mind."

Charlotte sat, fussing with the folds of her long skirt while she thought what to say. "It's about school," she began at last, thinking how well she had been reciting her lessons since a year ago March when she had made her mind up to apply herself to her studies, and how much she had enjoyed the pursuit of knowledge for its own sake. "Last year, when Aurora graduated from the eighth grade, she asked about going on with her schooling on the mainland and you said you wished you could send her, but it would cost too much for room and board. And even if you'd had the money, you couldn't let her go because you needed her help here with the sewing and the housekeeping, and to take charge of all the rest of us when you're tending the light."

Julia's rocking paused. She looked expectantly at Charlotte. "Go on. I'm listening." Both her chair, and her needle eased back into motion.

"Well, this year when Bridget graduates, she'll be happy to be done with school, but I won't feel that way next year when it's my turn. For a long time now, I've been trying to figure things out. It's been really hard since Papa died, but I know now what he would want me to do. I've just got to go on with my schooling!" She didn't mention her equally strong desire to leave South Manitou Island, to escape the one place that would always remind her of her father's passing.

Julia set her darning in her lap, pushed at one of the dark curls that fringed her forehead, then reached out for Charlotte, enfolding her daughter's slender hands inside her own chubby ones. "Charlotte, this is not easy for me, but I must be honest with you. I wish with all my heart I could send you off to the mainland next year so you could attend school. The Lord knows you'd do well enough. This year, you haven't brought home anything less than an A.

"But despite your good grades, I can't let you go. The truth is, I've had all I could do to keep up since your papa died. And after all the help you've been to me this year, I couldn't possibly manage without you!"

For the next few moments, both pride and resentment battled for a place in Charlotte's heart, finally giving way to disappointment.

Her mother continued. "I've seen a remarkable change in you over the last year, Charlotte, and I'm mighty proud of the way you've pitched in, working hard to keep the tower windows and stairs clean and spotless, and helping to show visitors around on weekends. Why, you know nearly as much about lightkeeping as I do, and when visitors come to see the tower room, they love to hear you tell how the lamp is lit, and the glass kept shiny. I'm sure this seems unfair, but the truth is, I must keep you here on the island for a few more years!"

Charlotte's dream shattered, like a tower window in the

path of a powerful Canadian goose during spring migration. It was as if shards of glass cut into her, piercing her heart.

Her mother continued holding her hands, gazing at her with watery eyes that said she was even more sorry than Charlotte over circumstances. Moments later, her mother released her and again took up her darning. "If I know you, Charlotte, once you make your mind up to do something, you won't let anything stop you, not even the fact that you live on this island. You'll find a way to accomplish the goals you set for yourself."

Charlotte was still contemplating the dilemma the following afternoon, a warm, breezy, partly sunny Saturday, as she ambled along the beach kicking pebbles into the water. She stopped to pick up a flat stone and gave it a side-armed toss, counting four skips before it sank.

Across the rippling azure waters of the crescent harbor, she counted two steamers taking on lumber at the town dock, and in the opposite direction, two schooners, white canvas billowing, as they sailed through the passage. From afar, a steam whistle pierced the air.

She munched on the last inch of the peppermint stick she'd been eating since she'd finished cleaning the watch room, and stared up at the changing shapes of the clouds. "Now what do I do, Papa? Mama says I can't leave the island."

To the rhythm of the waves lapping the shore was added the crunch of boot heels against stones. Charlotte turned to find Seth, a floppy planter's hat shading all but his lopsided grin. He carried two fishing poles, a bucket of worms, and the bashed-in straw hat he had given her the first time he'd taken her fishing two years ago.

He pressed the misshapen head covering over her toffee tresses with a pat. "Come on, Charlie. Chores are done. Let's go fishing in the little lake." He referred to the pond less than a mile away.

Charlotte managed a smile that quickly dissolved as she took her pole and followed him down the path inland.

Seth cast her a backward glance. "Something the matter? You're mighty pokey, and a sight quieter than usual." He waited for her to catch up to him.

"I thought I had things all figured out. Now I don't know what to do." She relayed her desire to go to the mainland to attend school, and the reasons her mother had given that made it impossible. "I'm sure Papa would want me to go on with my learning, but how can I do that if I can't leave South Manitou?"

Seth felt traitorous. He was glad Charlie's mother had said no to letting her daughter leave home. South Manitou just wouldn't be the same without her. Still, he respected Charlie's desire to continue her studies. She was bright and inquisitive and deserved a chance to pursue her dream. In a moment of contemplation, the perfect solution came to him. "Charlie, I believe your teacher, Mrs. Garrity, can help you earn your high school diploma right here on the island."

"But, how? Everyone on the island knows you can't go past the eighth grade here."

"Everyone on the island also knows she taught at Ann Arbor High School before her husband died. You're always telling me how much you like having Mrs. Garrity for a teacher. Folks say she's better than the teacher you had last year, or the one I had when I was still in school. They think Mrs. Garrity is the best to ever come here— that she spends all her time helping her students because she doesn't have children of her own. I haven't met her—not formally—but I've seen her about, and I don't believe folks are just talking through their hats. Why don't you ask if she'll be your tutor?"

Charlotte hated to give up on finding a way off the island, but the prospect of being tutored held great appeal. It also seemed too much to hope for. "I'll think it over," she promised, dreading the possibility that if she were to ask for help, her teacher might say no.

Despite hours of contemplation, Charlotte couldn't find the fortitude to approach Mrs. Garrity. She began each day with good intentions, but ended each afternoon walking away from the one-room schoolhouse without mentioning one word to her teacher. When she went to bed on Thursday night following nearly a week of anxiety over the situation, she made herself a promise that come Friday, she would find the courage to ask Mrs. Garrity to be her tutor.

She awoke to a splendid spring day. Her heart soared with new hope on the way to the schoolhouse in town. The day passed quickly for Charlotte, made particularly interesting by the news her teacher shared of the World's Columbian Exposition which had opened in Chicago on the first of the month.

Relatives of Mrs. Garrity from Detroit had sent literature, photographs, and newspaper clippings. Charlotte listened in wonder as her teacher read of the twenty-two carriages drawn by highstepping horses that paraded down Michigan Avenue carrying President Grover Cleveland, his cabinet, and the Spanish dignitaries. She was amazed to learn that hundreds of thousands of men, women and children gathered in the mud at the base of the platform beside the domed Administration Building, waiting for the president to set the Fair in motion at the touch of a golden button.

"Instantaneously," Mrs. Garrity read, "water gushed from the Columbian Fountain, flags were unfurled, colorful banners and streamers fluttered from buildings. At the same time, steam launches in the Grand Canal set off whistles, chimes rang from palaces, and cannons boomed from the *USS Michigan* in the harbor."

Charlotte could think of nothing more exciting than to see for herself how the rest of the world had come to Jackson Park, but in the six months during which the Fair would be open, she would consider herself fortunate to venture as far as Glen Arbor, let alone all the way to Chicago.

Too soon, it seemed, Mrs. Garrity finished with her news of the Fair and dismissed school for the weekend. Charlotte approached her teacher at the blackboard where the small, almost pretty woman who was a little past thirty, was washing off the day's lessons. Charlotte picked up a rag, dipped it in the bucket of water, and went to work alongside her, trying to dig up the courage to open the subject that had been on her mind these past several days.

"Thank you for your help, Charlotte. I'm surprised you stayed behind on such a fine day," Mrs. Garrity commented in the slightly quivering voice that, though normal for her, always made her sound a bit tense.

Now that the time had come for Charlotte to pose her question, she could hardly get her tongue to move. "I . . . I wondered if I could ask you about something, Mrs. Garrity?"

The teacher dropped her cloth in the bucket and turned to Charlotte, a questioning look in the dark brown eyes behind the gold-rimmed spectacles she sometimes wore. "Certainly. Let's sit down, shall we?" She motioned to the recitation bench.

Charlotte fidgeted with the cuff of her white cotton shirtwaist. The late afternoon sun slanted through the windows, glistening off the brilliants in the handle of the sword pin on her teacher's high collar. Mrs. Garrity waited patiently, her mouth curved in a half-smile.

"Mrs. Garrity—" Charlotte swallowed and wet her lips. "I really like school. I don't want to stop learning after I finish eighth grade next year. I asked my mother about going away to school, but she needs me on the Island. So . . . a friend said I should ask if you could help me study at home."

Mrs. Garrity looked her straight in the eye. "If you're really serious about this, you would have to put in long hours of study each day. Would you be willing to do that?"

Charlotte's gaze never faltered. "Yes, I would."

Taking a deep breath, Mrs. Garrity glanced briefly away, then fixed on her pupil an almost heavenly expression. "In that case, Charlotte, I would be delighted to help you. You are one of my very best—rather, you are *the* best, hardest-working student in this school. Do you have any specific goals planned? Entrance to a university, perhaps?"

"I hadn't really—"

She flicked her hand. "We have plenty of time to decide that later. For now, it's enough that you want to continue your schooling. You're already half a year ahead of yourself, you know. You'll probably be ready for your eighth grade exams by January, if you continue to work hard. Then, if you will help me with my schoolroom chores, I will have the time to tutor you privately."

Charlotte's heart nearly burst with happiness. The generosity of her teacher's offer seemed overwhelming. "I'll do anything you ask, Mrs. Garrity. Anything at all!"

"Even come to school early on a cold winter's morning and kindle a fire in the stove?"

"Oh, yes! I'd be happy to do it!"

"And would you be willing to hear the younger students with their lessons at the front of the room while I work with the older ones at the back?"

"Yes, of course!"

"Then we have struck a bargain!"

Charlotte stood abruptly. "I can't wait to tell Mama the good news! Good-bye, Mrs. Garrity! I'll see you Monday!" On winged feet, she took off down the aisle and out the back door. She was halfway across the schoolyard when she heard her teacher call to her.

"Charlotte! Wait!" Mrs. Garrity was standing on the schoolhouse step.

Charlotte came running back. "Yes, Mrs. Garrity? What is it?"

"I have a question for you. Do you mind coming inside for a moment? It requires a little explanation."

Charlotte followed her indoors. This time, Mrs. Garrity went straight to her desk, pulling a chair alongside for Charlotte. A letter lay on top of the news clippings of the Fair. Mrs. Garrity spoke as she glanced over the gold embossed stationery covered with the fluid strokes of fine penmanship.

"My relatives have invited me to visit the Fair with them in July. They want me to bring a friend." She focused on Charlotte. "Would you like to come with me?"

Charlotte's mouth dropped open. Though her mind shouted, "Yes, yes, yes!" she couldn't get her throat to work.

"You needn't worry about expenses," Mrs. Garrity added.

Mute with euphoric shock, Charlotte finally put her hand over her mouth.

Mrs. Garrity tilted her head. "Are you feeling all right, Charlotte? You look quite pale."

She managed to coax her jaw back into action. "All right? . . . All right? . . . Mrs. Garrity, I haven't felt this all right since I was born!"

Mrs. Garrity leaned back, letting out her high-pitched trill of a laugh. "Well, thank goodness for that. You looked as though you might faint dead away, and I would have to resort to smelling salts. I take it you are interested in joining me, then?"

"Interested? I can hardly wait!"

"Then there's just one last consideration. I'll have to talk to your mother to settle the details. When would be a good time for me to call on her? I know her duties at the lighthouse keep her busy."

"Why don't you stop by tonight after the evening meal, if that's convenient?"

"Seven o'clock?"

"I'll tell Mama to expect you. Be sure to come around to the side door. Mama wouldn't want me bringing company in through her kitchen."

"The side door, seven o'clock. I'll see you then, Charlotte."

Charlotte set her feet on a course straight for home. The moment she stepped into the basement kitchen, she told her mother of the impending visit, and began helping her to prepare dinner. Afterward, she wiped and put away the dishes and tidied up the sitting room, which was never really messy due to the possibility of inspection at any time. Nevertheless, Charlotte made certain every speck of dust was banished from the mantel, tables, chairs, and window sills. She set the books in the portable library in order, and scrutinized the ivory plaster walls for marks, fingerprints, or smudges. With the carpet sweeper, she eliminated any dust that might be hiding in the braided oval rug, then draped a clean rag over a broom handle and chased cobwebs from the corners of the ceiling. She had put away the sweeper and dust rags and broom and was checking the antimacassars on the sofa for stains, when the mantel clock struck seven, and Mrs. Garrity's knock sounded on the sitting room door.

CHAPTER 4

Charlotte invited Mrs. Garrity into the sitting room, offering her a seat on the sofa, while her mother served her coffee along with some freshly baked oatmeal raisin cookies. Charlotte felt very self-conscious having her teacher here in her very own home, and was keenly aware of certain details she had never noticed in the schoolroom, such as the little lace gloves she removed and laid in her lap, and her navy blue dress with a bodice of tucks and pleats which Charlotte hadn't seen before.

After the initial pleasantries had been exchanged, Mrs. Garrity spoke to Charlotte's mother about the topic foremost on everyone's mind. "I'm sure Charlotte has told you I have invited her to the World's Columbian Exposition. I want you to know that my relatives will provide accommodations aboard their private yacht, the *Martha G. Robert's*—" She fidgeted with the napkin in her lap, then went on. "My late husband's brother makes frequent trips between Detroit, Mackinac Island, and Chicago this time of year. He'll be stopping at South Manitou on July fifth, then going on to the Fair for a week. All of Charlotte's expenses will be taken care of, and I will be with her from the time we leave, until we return. I hope these arrangements meet with your approval, Mrs. Richards."

While Mrs. Garrity had been talking, Charlotte had noticed Seth in the front hallway outside the sitting room door. She hoped he hadn't discovered the oatmeal cookies still sitting on the tray in front of her. They were his favorites, and it would be just like him to invite himself into the meeting just to get more in addition to the three he had already eaten for dessert.

Julia sipped her coffee, then set her cup and saucer aside. "You've made my daughter a very generous offer, Mrs. Garrity. I'm not certain why such an honor has come her way, but I'm thrilled for her!" Turning to her daughter, she added, "You know what a trip like this means, Charlotte. You will be away from home without me for the very first time, and you must be on your best behavior every minute."

"Yes, Mama, I will," Charlotte quickly assured her.

"Good. Now maybe Mrs. Garrity will give us some advice as to what you should pack for your trip."

Seth had finished his work at the fog signal building and was sitting on the stoop at the side door, watching the vaporous air move in from the west. His father had set the whistle to blowing, and he listened carefully to the blasts for any irregularity, knowing the cantankerous equipment, along with his father, would require his assistance at the first sign of trouble. After several minutes of perfectly timed whistle blasts, Charlotte and her teacher emerged from the sitting room.

Seth sprang to his feet, pushing the planter's hat back

on his head. "Good evening, ladies."

"Mrs. Garrity, do you know Seth Trevelyn?" Charlotte asked.

"We've met in passing. Pleased to meet you, Seth."

"My pleasure, ma'am. Can I walk you ladies to the gate?"

Mrs. Garrity nodded. "How kind of you."

With a flair Charlotte had never seen in Seth before, he offered an arm to each of them and walked them down the path. "I was at the fog signal building earlier, helping Papa build a fire for the boiler, when he reminded me how much the evening seemed like fall. That set me to thinking about a treat you ladies might enjoy." He reached into each of his pockets. "An apple for the teacher, and one for her student. Fresh from the storage pit!"

"I had forgotten all about these," Charlotte admitted, remembering how at harvest time last year, she had painstakingly helped Seth wrap dozens of apples in corn husks and bury them deep in the ground below the frost line. She sank her teeth into the crisp fruit. "This is just as good as the day we picked it!"

"This will sustain me on my walk home," said Mrs. Garrity as Seth opened the gate for her. "Thank you for a pleasant evening, both of you!"

Charlotte waved good-bye, then turned toward the house, falling in step with Seth as she chattered excitedly. "Mrs. Garrity says we're going to the Fair for a whole week, beginning July fifth!"

"I know all about it," Seth claimed. "You're going on a private yacht called the *Martha G*."

"How did you know?" Charlotte demanded. Then a thought struck her. "You were listening from the hallway, weren't you?"

The corner of his mouth tilted upward. "And it's a mighty good thing, too. You don't know what you're getting into, going on that yacht with Mrs. Garrity's kinfolks."

"What do you mean?"

"They're bound to be pretty fancy company for an ordinary island girl like you."

Seth's words stung. "Are you trying to tell me I'm not good enough for them?"

"I didn't say that at all. I'm just warning you. Mrs. Garrity's relatives are mighty rich, and rich folks are different. You won't know how to talk, or act, or eat with the likes of them. Besides, you can't sit still more than a few minutes at a time. Before you know it, you'll be getting yourself into all sorts of trouble on that boat!"

"I will not, Seth Trevelyn! And I don't care if they *are* rich. I'll get along with them just fine!" Charlotte ran away from him as fast as she could, to the keeper's quarters and up to her room. She grabbed her dolly from the foot of her bed and flopped onto the quilt. Rolling onto her back, she held the doll away from her, looking squarely into her button eyes. "I don't care what Seth says, I'm going to have a good time on my trip," she promised.

Seth had been fishing at his favorite hole at the pond for over an hour, but still Charlotte had not shown up after school as she had promised to—for the third time this month. And it was only the fourth of June!

He baited and dropped her line into the pond, wedging the pole against a log with a rock. After two nibbles on her line, her hook had been eaten clean by sunfish, and he rebaited it.

He was thinking how the fish ignored his own line entirely when he noticed another tiny tug on Charlotte's. After a moment, he picked up her pole and gave a jerk to set her hook. Instead of the perch he was hoping to land, her hook came flying, empty, out of the water. "Blamed pumpkin seeds!" he said, referring to the sunfish that infested the small lake. "You've had all the dinner you're gonna get from me today."

Disgusted, he picked up Charlotte's pole and his own, slung them over his shoulder and pulled down his hat, taking off in the direction of home. When he intersected with the path that led from the schoolhouse, he heard Charlotte calling to him.

"Seth! Wait up!" She came running from the direction of the school. "I'm sorry I didn't meet you like I promised," she apologized, catching her breath. "I stayed after—"

"To help Mrs. Garrity," he finished for her.

"We were decorating the schoolhouse for graduation tomorrow night. We put up streamers and a banner. And we were talking about our trip to the Fair. Mrs. Garrity said there's a whole building there built by women all over the world. She said a woman designed it, and everything inside was made by women. Do you know what else she said?"

"'Mrs. Garrity said, Mrs. Garrity said,'" he mimicked. "You stay after school to help her, and when you're done, she's all you talk about. I'm beginning to wish I'd never heard of Mrs. Garrity!" He strode off, fishing poles bouncing on his shoulder.

Charlotte continued toward home, puzzling out Seth's

behavior. "If I didn't know you better, Seth Trevelyn, I'd say you're jealous of Mrs. Garrity."

Charlotte went to bed early, but she was too excited about her departure the next day to feel drowsy. In the still of the evening, a night hawk circled outside her window, sending out his nasal *peent* each time he swept the ground. On the beach below, a killdeer told its name and issued a scolding. One of the barn cats was probably too close to its nest.

The distant boom of the Independence Day fireworks in town occasionally punctuated nature's melody. Everyone else from the keeper's quarters, except her mother who was on watch, had gone to see the display, but Charlotte had chosen to stay home, realizing she needed extra sleep before her big day.

The tower lamp sent a pale wash against the wall where the closet door stood open. Just inside hung the new skirt Aurora had made her. It almost brushed the ground when Charlotte put it on. Since it was the first long skirt she'd had, it would take some getting used to.

Charlotte recognized her mother's footfalls on the stairs, causing the third tread from the top to creak. She paused at the bedroom door.

"Come in, Mama. I'm still awake."

There was something comforting in the soft swish of her mother's cotton petticoats as she crossed the room, and the muffled grating of her corset stays when she bent to sit down in the rocker. She laid a knotted handkerchief in her lap and pulled a wrinkled one from her sleeve to daub her upper lip, then tucked it back in place. "I wanted to talk with you before your sisters came home from the fireworks." She considered the tiny bundle for a few seconds, then, reaching for Charlotte's hand, placed it against her palm and wrapped her fingers around it, squeezing them before letting go.

Without even looking, Charlotte could tell the parcel held several dollars in coins, a veritable fortune where her family was concerned.

"For a long while, I've been putting money by, a little at a time. I want you to have some of it to spend at the Fair."

Charlotte worked the knot loose. Inside the handkerchief lay one five-dollar gold piece, and two silver dollars. She handed it back. "It's too much, Mama. I couldn't possibly—"

"Buy something nice for each of your sisters and brothers, and for yourself. The opportunity won't come but this once."

Charlotte tucked the five-dollar gold piece beneath her pillow, handed back the silver dollars, then lay on her side facing her mother. "Mama, if you could have anything you wanted from the Fair, what would it be?"

"Don't you go spending on me, now. That's not the point. The money's to be spent on you children. Mind what I say."

"I will, Mama. But if you *could*, what would you fancy?"

Contemplatively, Julia set her chair to rocking. On the third trip over the chair's runners, she answered, "I'd fancy having you home safe again, Charlotte."

Except for the solemn manner in which the words were spoken, to Charlotte the answer sounded perfectly silly. "Mama, sometimes you're mighty hard to figure."

Julia paused, brushing a wisp of a curl from her daughter's forehead. "When you're grown, you'll understand. Now, it's time for you to get some rest. You've an awfully big day ahead of you. Sleep tight, dear."

"'Night, Mama."

Charlotte rose in darkness, did her chores, and at first light, ran up to the tower. Sometime overnight, the *Martha G.* must have slipped into the protective arms of the island, for when she scanned the harbor, there was the motor yacht Mrs. Garrity had told her to watch for. It had a black smokestack and two masts rising from the pristine white hull that was riding at anchor on the quiet blue-green surface of the lake.

She burst into the kitchen where her mother was scrambling a skilletful of eggs. "It's here, Mama—the yacht Mrs. Garrity told me about! I've got to get Seth and Mr. Trevelyn to hitch up the wagon, and bring down my bag, and—"

"Calm down, will you, child?" Julia said, scraping eggs onto a huge serving platter that was already laden with browned sausage. "Breakfast first. Take this up to the dining table, will you? And call the others."

Charlotte took hold of the warm, heavy platter with potholders and carried it upstairs, then went out on the stoop and rang the bell. Mr. Trevelyn came in from the tower, and Nat and Seth from the barn in what seemed like record time.

No one lingered over a second cup of coffee this morning. By the time the wagon was hitched, the yacht was making its way to the dock.

Mrs. Garrity was ready and waiting when the wagon arrived. Mr. Trevelyn drove onto the dock all the way to the end where the yacht was making its approach, then helped Charlotte and her teacher down.

A portly man with a captain's hat shoved back on his head and a fat cigar in his teeth watched as his pilot made the approach. He stood on the aft deck, one glistening white shoe propped on the gunwale beneath the side rails. His unruly lambchop sideburns, waxed handlebar mustache, and bushy eyebrows that shot off on angles like wings gave a wild countenance to his ruddy face.

When the vessel was near enough, two deck hands leaped off with lines, ready to make fast. No sooner had the bumpers on the hull made contact with the dock than the robust man dropped the gangway and let out with a gravelly, "Helen Garrity, my but you're a welcome sight! Come aboard and give your old brother-in-law a proper welcome!"

Helen's complexion colored as a grin widened on her pretty mouth. "Hello, George! You're looking mighty fine yourself," Helen replied, taking Charlotte by the elbow to lead her aboard.

Helen Garrity made introductions. "Charlotte, my brother-in-law, Mr. George Garrity. George, this is Miss Charlotte Richards, my traveling companion."

He let out a huge puff from his cigar, then flicked the ash, letting it fall onto the beautiful red, gold and cream Persian carpet that covered the highly varnished mahogany deck. "Pleased to make your acquaintance, Miss Richards." His huge hand engulfed hers, pumping her arm so hard she feared it would came apart at the elbow. At the same time, he plugged the cigar into his mouth again and emitted a stream of smoke angled to blow downwind of her.

Even so, "Mr. Garrity," was all she could manage

before the stench of his disgusting habit overcame her, sending her into a coughing fit.

Almost in sympathy, George himself began to cough, a loose, rumbling, congested sound that gained momentum over the next several seconds.

"You know, George, you really ought to give up those nasty things," scolded Helen, taking the cigar from him and dropping it over the rail before he had regained control of his heaving chest.

Loudly, he cleared the phlegm from his throat. He spit over the side, hauled out the largest white handkerchief Charlotte had ever seen to wipe his mouth, then turned to Helen, a look of contrition in his sparkling gray eyes as he stuffed the wad of cotton back into the front pocket of his double-breasted blue blazer. "I've given up this habit a thousand times. I do make it a point never to smoke while eating or sleeping. Or, while kissing a pretty young teacher. How 'bout a kiss for this nasty relative of yours?" He bent slightly, offering her his bushy cheek.

She stood back. "Now, George, you know I don't cotton to such public displays of affection."

In a twinkling of an eye, George had captured Helen's face in his huge hands and landed a loud, smacking kiss on her forehead. Afterward, he let loose with a rip-roaring laugh.

Helen colored deeply, shaking her finger at him. "George, you haven't changed an iota since I saw you last."

"You haven't changed much either, 'cept maybe to get a little better-looking since I left you off here last fall. I sure hated to do it, but island life seems to have agreed with you." His attention shifted briefly to Seth, who was helping a deck hand carry aboard his sister-in-law's trunk, then back to Helen.

"Say, don't know any fellas on the island, here, who'd want to go along on this trip, do you? A strong one who's not afraid of hard work? Some experience in steam boilers would be a plus. Had to put one of my crew off at Mackinac Island. You know how lake men can toss down the whiskey when they're on shore leave. Now I'm shorthanded."

Helen nodded in Seth's direction. "He knows steam boilers from working the lighthouse fog signal."

George Garrity wasted not even a moment pondering Helen's recommendation. "Say, you there!"

Seth's head snapped up.

"Yes, you! What's your name, young fellow?"

"Trevelyn, sir. Seth Trevelyn." Seth shifted the weight of the trunk from his right hand to his left, wondering what Mrs. Garrity had packed to make it so heavy.

George came up beside him, looking him straight in the eye. "Seth Trevelyn, how would you like to hire on with George Garrity for a fortnight? I'll pay you a dollar and a quarter a day, and a bonus of five dollars plus a day off to spend it at the Fair. What do you say?"

Seth could hardly believe his ears. He glanced at his father who was waiting for him on the seat of the wagon. Mr. Trevelyn gave a nod of approval.

"I'd like that, sir. I'd like that very much."

George thrust out his hand. "It's a bargain, then. Go on down below. See Stokes. He'll outfit ya, assign you a bunk, show you the ropes."

It was all Seth could do to keep the trunk steady in his left hand while shaking with his right. "Yes, sir. Thank you, sir."

"No need to thank me. I'll get my money's worth out of ya before you see this port again."

As Seth disappeared down the narrow passage stairs, John began working his team to turn them around. George called out to him, "Mr. Trevelyn, I'll take your son off this island a lad, and deliver him back safe and sound, a man. That's a promise from George Garrity you can count on."

Mr. Trevelyn doffed his hat. "I'll hold you to it, Mr. Garrity."

Charlotte could hardly believe Seth would be aboard for the entire trip, and that he would earn so much money. Quickly she calculated his pay—six days at a dollar and a quarter plus the five dollar bonus—twelve dollars and fifty cents. In a week's time, he would earn a small fortune. She bet he was glad now that he had heard of Mrs. Garrity!

She fingered the half eagle in the handkerchief she had pinned inside her skirt pocket. Her mother had saved a long time for it, but Seth would have as much just handed to him! Seth was right, with money flowing so freely, the rich *did* see things differently than she did. She wondered what else she would discover about the Garritys that set them apart from an ordinary island girl like herself.

CHAPTER 5

"Charlotte, this is Mrs. Martha Garrity, George's mother, from Detroit. Mother Garrity, Miss Charlotte Richards, my traveling companion." Charlotte's teacher made the introduction on the aft deck as the boat pulled away from the dock.

The elder Mrs. Garrity's silver-streaked dark hair was caught up beneath a wide-brimmed bonnet with a huge, bright pink satin flower in the front. Overlaying the creation was a sheer pink silk scarf tied off to the side in a bouffant bow. The headgear detracted from the pointiness of her long nose, the jut of her angular chin, and the close-set, penetrating nature of small blue eyes that had tried to turn brown in one spot on her left iris.

Charlotte offered her hand to the woman in the white wicker chair. "Pleased to meet you, ma'am."

Martha's white cotton glove brushed Charlotte's bare fingertips feigning a handshake, then returned to the book that lay open on her lap.

"Charlotte, make yourself comfortable." Her teacher indicated a wicker chair across from Martha. "Once we're underway, I'll show you your cabin. Maybe you'd like something to read." She pulled a recent issue of *Harper's Weekly* from a selection of magazines on the small wicker table beside Martha, took up a copy of *Atlantic Monthly* for herself, and sat on the other side of her relative.

"Really, Helen, I was expecting your companion to be more your age. Why, she's a mere schoolgirl!"

"So she is," Helen admitted, "but an intelligent, studious young woman with a desire to attend university one day."

Charlotte inwardly flinched at the part about university. She still hadn't decided where her education would lead.

"Oh?" Martha's tone conveyed an abundance of skepticism. "Is her father an alumnus of the University of Michigan?"

Charlotte put down the magazine she had been pretending to read, forced her mouth to curve upward at the corners, and fastened her eyes on the elder Mrs. Garrity's. "No, ma'am, he was not. However, I do not believe my admission will be denied because I lack for a relative who has attended there."

"Perhaps not, but you had better plan to make high scores on your admissions exams. There is no room at that institution for the average scholar. They are top achievers, all."

Helen nodded in agreement. "Of course you are right, Mother Garrity. Charlotte is an excellent student, the best in her class. I think she stands a very good chance of gaining entrance. But enough about school matters. How have you been faring since we last saw one another?"

Helen and her mother-in-law lapsed into a conversation about life in Detroit where, much to Charlotte's surprise,

Martha said she had been spending much of her time preparing for a charity bazaar for the Protestant Orphan Asylum. As the conversation continued about relatives and friends unfamiliar to Charlotte, her eyes and her mind strayed.

She couldn't help being impressed by the luxuriousness of the yacht's appointments. The afterdeck, though casual, was furnished with a fine walnut and glass table. On it stood a cut crystal bowl overflowing with freshly cut pink tea roses. The deck's perimeter was surrounded by a double brass rail, shiny enough to use as a mirror. It extended forward from the afterdeck along an exterior passageway.

Charlotte slipped out of her chair and stepped up to the rail where the prevailing northwesterly wind brought cool, clear air from Upper Michigan across the northern reaches of the lake to the Manitou Passage. As the boat left the harbor and turned southwesterly between the island and the mainland, she saw crewmen making ready to hoist sails on the two masts, one forward and the other aft of the center smokestack, but she didn't see any sign of Seth among them, and wondered where he had gone.

Behind her was a door. Curiosity drew her inside, where she found an interior passageway that was lined with polished mahogany cabin doors on each side. The brass name plates attached read: "Detroit," "Ann Arbor," "Flint," "Lansing," "Grand Rapids," "Kalamazoo," and farthest forward on the port side door at the end of the passageway, "Michigan." From there, a set of very narrow stairs led to the next lower level. As she descended, extremely warm air stinking of machine oil greeted her, as did the loud *thunk, thunk, thunk* of the steam engine that sent vibrations into the soles of her laced boots, through her very bones.

Seth had been sent below, and Charlotte would not rest until she found him and learned what he was doing that was worth a dollar and a quarter a day to George Garrity.

One of the deck crew told Seth he could find Stokes either at the controls in the engine room or the furnace in the boiler room. The stairs below gave Seth entrance to the engine compartment, dark and noisy and reeking of machine oil. The smell reminded him of the fog signal building, where he had spent many hours lubricating the light service equipment.

Stokes wasn't in sight, but an oil lamp lit the narrow passage forward to the boiler and furnace. When Seth first laid eyes on his new foreman, he began to wonder whether he had really been fortunate in hiring on with George Garrity, or if foolish would more aptly apply.

Except for the grimy black soot from his belly button to the top of his balding head, his new boss was bare from the waist up. Though every bit as big as Garrity, in place of rolls of fat that covered the yacht's owner, Stokes had muscles that bulged from biceps and forearms, chest and neck. Even his cheeks and jaws looked as tough as carved leather in the red glow of the furnace flames. The only sign of physical deterioration was the beginning of a pot belly.

Seth came up behind Stokes, who was feeding the fire, shoveling coal from a huge bunker into the open door of the firebox where bright orange-yellow flames licked and leaped.

"Pardon me, Mr. Stokes!" Seth bellowed out to make himself heard above the din of the throbbing engine. "Mr. Garrity just hired me on and told me to report to you."

Stokes clanked shut the heavy iron door of the furnace and turned to face Seth, the whites of his eyes contrasting sharply with the black smudges on his wide cheeks and broad forehead. "What the Sam Hill? I asked Old Man Garrity to hire on another hand and what does he send me? A mere lad!" he shouted, his gruff voice rising above the clamor of the machinery.

"You just show me what you want done," said Seth, lowering the pitch of his voice, while raising its volume. "I can work as hard as any man you've got!" He knew he shouldn't boast, but he couldn't let Stokes hold his youth against him.

"Oh? Is that right, kid?" Stokes boomed, a huge white grin emerging above his blackened chin. "Did Mr. Garrity tell you what your job was?"

"No, sir."

Stokes crossed his arms on his massive chest. "It's anything I say it is. I'm chief engineer. When I give you an order, you do what I say, and you do it *now*. Understood, kid?"

"Yes, sir! And my name's Seth, not 'kid.'"

"Now get out of here, k—Seth. Go up to the fo'c'sle. You'll find a pair of overalls on one of the bunks. That's your bunk, and your duds. Put 'em on and report back, pronto. I need you to stoke the furnace."

Seth wasted not a second making his way up from the hot depths. A cabin steward told him how to find the crew's quarters forward of the foremast. Very little of the ninety-foot long motor yacht was designated to the bunks. Four of them lined the bulkhead in two tiers, narrowing toward the bow. His was on the top level. A large, dark-skinned fellow occupied the bunk below. Within two minutes Seth had stripped off his shirt and pants and slipped on the pinstriped overalls, pulling the straps over his bare shoulders and across his chest to fasten them at the waist. In another thirty seconds, he was again descending the stairs to the hot furnace room.

Stokes gave him a pair of heavy gloves. "Put these on and get to work firing the furnace. When I holler, you stop. You'll be fueling for about ten or fifteen minutes at a time. During breaks, you can stick your head out the porthole for some air." With a nod, he indicated a starboard opening through which a fresh breeze could blow. "Now, I'm goin' back to my controls."

Seth dug into the black pile with vigor, dusting himself and his new overalls with soot which quickly liquefied on contact with his sweaty skin. The dryness of the hot air, however, evaporated the moisture as soon as it beaded on his skin. As he lifted shovelful after shovelful of coal into the furnace, he wondered how many hours would pass before someone came to relieve him.

Halfway down the steps, Charlotte's eyes adjusted to the darkness well enough to make out the heavy machinery that was responsible for the deafening noise—pistons and rods pumping forcefully, looking as though they could swallow up anyone who came too near, and smelly enough to warn off a more delicate soul. A huge man, busy with an oil can, had his back to her. She hurried down the last few steps and skirted past him and through a narrow space in the machine-cluttered chamber.

Her long skirt caught on a metal protrusion. She tugged on it, but it wouldn't come free. Again and again she tried to loosen the fabric. Finally, she yanked hard. It tore at the hem. A queasy feeling shot through her. She had worn the new skirt Aurora had made especially for her only a few hours and already it was damaged. At least the rip was confined mostly to the underside and would hardly show when mended. She would fix it as soon as Mrs. Garrity took her to her cabin, but first, she must find Seth.

Seth bent his energy to his work, keeping a steady pace, dropping load after load of fuel into the huge fire. Once, he glimpsed a flash of white between the boilers, then told himself he must have imagined it. Maybe the heat was making him see things. He'd never felt this hot before, or this thirsty. He'd been working less than a half hour, but his arms were feeling the strain of the task.

When he straightened to give his back a moment's rest, he thought he was imagining Charlie's familiar face in front of him, then he realized she was actually there in the flesh.

"How do you like your new job, Seth?" she shouted, a silly, innocent grin on her face, turned ruddy from the heat.

The sight of her sent a flash of anger hotter than the furnace through Seth's veins, followed by a chill of fear for her safety. "Charlie, what in the world are you doing down here? Don't you know this is no place for a girl?" He swung shut the furnace door, whipped off his filthy glove, and took her firmly by the elbow to guide her away from the dangerous place.

Seth's grip sent a painful jolt through her. She twisted and writhed. "Let go! You're hurting my arm!"

"I'll hurt a lot more than your arm if you ever come down here again!" Seth warned, nearly losing his hold on her.

From behind Charlie, Stokes's voice boomed, "What's going on here? Get back to work, kid!"

Seth drew a breath to protest, but Stokes cut him short. "Now!"

Seth dropped Charlie's elbow and returned to the furnace.

"Come with me, pretty miss." Stokes didn't sound particularly annoyed as he led Charlie away. He even let loose with a belly laugh over something Charlie told him.

Soon enough, the gruff boss returned. "Hey kid! The next time that silly young lady friend of yours shows up down here, you're fired! Now, start fueling the furnace!" With that, Stokes turned and lumbered back to the boiler.

Seth lifted his shovel and set to work, praying Charlie wouldn't wander below again before he got off duty and could warn her to stay clear.

Three and a half hours later, Seth dragged himself up to the crew's quarters. He had instructions from Stokes to awaken the man who was to replace him on duty. Buck, he had been told, occupied the bunk below his. He was the only other crew member in the fo'c'sle, still sound asleep, just as he had been when Seth had come in to put on his overalls.

After several attempts, Seth managed to arouse Buck and send him to the boiler room. Eager to clean up, Seth located the crew's wash room, a tiny compartment with a toilet and sink, just aft of the fo'c'sle. His whole body ached, his throat was parched, and he smelled worse than he'd ever smelled in his life—wreaking of soot and oil and sweat that had dried on his skin. All he wanted to do was drop onto his bunk and stay until someone turned him out for his next duty, but he couldn't possibly go to sleep now, not until he had found Charlie.

After ten minutes at the wash basin, he realized no amount of scrubbing would rid him of the coal soot that had embedded itself into his skin.

He went back to the fo'c'sle and changed from his overalls into the pants and shirt he'd been wearing when he'd come aboard, then stepped out into the passageway. If he didn't find Charlie soon, Stokes would settle his hash but good.

CHAPTER 6

When Charlotte took luncheon with the Garritys in the main saloon, no one seemed to notice the damaged hem of her skirt. Soon after she had finished her strawberry shortcake, more conversation about people whom she didn't know caused her attention to wander. She excused herself from the damask-covered table to browse through the books in the cherry cabinet at the opposite end of the room. On her way, she took time to admire the saloon's luxurious appointments—the midnight blue velvet upholstery on a divan at the port side, a small Eakins painting hanging above, and the rosebud engraving on the silver lamp fixture beside it. The Garritys seemed perfectly at ease in these surroundings, but Charlotte couldn't imagine such expensive accouterments being part of her world at the lighthouse, where the fanciest piece of furniture was the canopied bed in which her mother slept.

Even the book cabinet, inset with small diamond-shaped panes of beveled glass, was a class above anything she had seen. It made the traveling lighthouse library, which she had always cherished, seem plainer than plain by comparison. She opened the bookcase, immediately enthralled and amazed at the assortment of titles that awaited her there, including sea stories by Herman Melville and Richard Henry Dana, Jr., the politics of John Adams and Abraham Lincoln, poetry by Longfellow, Dickinson, and several British authors. She chose a first-edition copy of Keats.

She had scanned the first half dozen pages when a breath of cool air came in from the port side. Looking up, she discovered Seth peeking in the door that joined the passageway.

He put a finger to his lips, then motioned for her to follow him. She returned the book to its rightful place, closed the cabinet, and slipped out of the saloon.

"I see you've come up from Hades," she teased. "Why so secretive?"

He took her firmly by the wrist and led her forward, stopping just outside the entrance to the fo'c'sle. Through the slits of his hazel eyes, he addressed her sternly, but quietly. "Charlie Richards, don't you *ever* come down to the boiler room again, or I will personally see to it that you don't sit down for a week. What on earth did you think you were doing, wandering down there, anyway?"

Before she could answer, he continued his angry tirade. "Of all the crazy, thoughtless things you have done, that beats all. You could have been hurt, and hurt bad. Besides that, you nearly got me dismissed from my position with Mr. Garrity. I don't know why Mrs. Garrity invited you on her trip to the Fair, anyway. Someone should have told her your curious, gypsy-like nature would land you in trouble!"

Charlotte bristled at the stinging accusation, replying vehemently, though *soto voce*. "Seth Trevelyn, you're about the meanest person I ever met! Stokes wasn't nearly as upset as you are about finding me in the boiler room. And if you haven't figured it out, Mrs. Garrity asked me on this trip because she likes my company." Taking hold of her skirt, she turned away with a flourish, the heels of her high-topped shoes clicking purposefully as she made her way aft. Halfway astern, she heard the fo'c'sle door close.

With its quiet click, another thought popped into her head. Abruptly, she did an about face and marched back to the door. Since she could see no reason why she and Seth had spoken so quietly, she pounded on it furiously. From behind the thick mahogany panel, she could hear the voice of a crewman shouting derogatory remarks to the individual who was responsible for disturbing his peace. Until then, it hadn't occurred to her that anyone but Seth might be occupying the cabin, trying to rest. What would she do if an angry stranger answered her summons?

Panic swept through her, abating the instant Seth's scowling countenance appeared between the jamb and the partly opened door. Putting her face close to his, she ground out, "And one more thing, Seth Trevelyn, don't you *ever* call me Charlie again!"

Feeling the euphoria of having cast a longtime burden off her chest, even if it was the hundredth time in the last three years that she had warned Seth against calling her by the dreaded nickname, Charlotte fairly floated aft through the narrow passage, her own forceful words replaying themselves triumphantly in her mind.

She quietly returned to the bookcase. The Garritys were still talking, just as they were when she had left. She mindlessly turned the delicate rice paper pages of a red leatherbound volume. She was still reveling in her verbal victory when voices from the other end of the room seemed to take on a more emphatic tone, drawing her back to reality.

"Helen, I simply don't understand why you have taken yourself off to that desolate little island," said the elder Mrs. Garrity. "How long do you intend to stay?"

"I hadn't really thought about it. Another year, at the least, perhaps several years," Helen said casually.

Her mother-in-law clucked disapprovingly. "Surely you find no company of suitable economic and social standing there."

Charlotte could feel her cheeks burning at the insult. South Manitou Island was anything but desolate, with its dozen farms, scores of summer residents who came from Chicago and other points south each year, and the constant flow of lake boats during the shipping season.

And were the island's farmers and lightkeepers really inferior to city folk? Surely her teacher had never made her feel that way. She continued to listen, keeping her back to the woman who had so offended her.

"Mark my words, Helen," Martha continued, "you'll go through the woods and pick up a crooked stick at the last."

"Now, Mother, watch what you say," warned George. "No need to be so critical of Helen's new home."

"I'm only concerned about Helen. She hasn't been quite herself since Robert's passing last year. I'm not sure life on an isolated island is a wise thing for her."

"You are quite a dear to be so concerned about me, Mother," Helen's well-modulated voice was quiet, but still audible to Charlotte. "Heaven knows, I don't want to cause you any worry. I only hope you understand that I didn't go to South Manitou Island with the intention of 'picking up a stick,' as it were. I simply went there to discover what Robert had described as the most peaceful place on earth, and to find some solace in it."

"I never could understand why Robert went to that place," Martha admitted with disdain.

"No, I suppose not," Helen said wistfully. "Now, if you'll excuse me, I think I had better see to my guest."

Charlotte pretended to be reading the book she was holding when her teacher came up behind her. "Charlotte, perhaps you would like to see your cabin now. You can take Burns with you, if you like."

Until then, she hadn't even noted the author of the book. She carefully closed the volume. "I think I'll come back to it later," she decided, returning it to its place on the shelf.

"I think you'll like your accommodations," said her teacher, leading the way to the cabins. "There's a bookshelf with books chosen especially for you, and some prints and maps and other items related to your cabin's theme. Dinner will be served at half past six." When she came to the Michigan cabin, she opened the door and allowed Charlotte to enter ahead of her.

Charlotte stepped over the threshold into a room paneled in pine with hundreds of fascinating knots on walls and ceiling. Beneath her feet was an oval hooked rug, patterned after a map of the state as rendered by an early cartographer, with misshapen mitt and surrounding lakes showing designations of various ports and rivers. Even the important islands were represented, including South and North Manitou and Mackinac. The rug protected the highly polished floor, squares of maple fitted together in a basketweave design.

Partially covering the interesting knots that peppered the walls were the hangings of which Mrs. Garrity had spoken—decorative hand-colored maps, portraits of famous Michigan men, certificates, documents, and even currency all neatly framed and arranged in interesting groups.

"I'll leave you now to do your unpacking and getting settled in. I'll be just down the hall in the Ann Arbor room if you need me. Remember, dinner at half past six in the main saloon." She crossed the cabin to the clock hanging above the built-in desk and moved the long hand ahead by two minutes. "There. It's a little fast, but Mother Garrity is a stickler for promptness. She's been known to refuse seating to those who came late, even if it's only by a few minutes."

"I'll be on time," Charlotte promised.

"Bring an appetite. She never orders less than seven courses for her evening meal."

Charlotte was about to close her door when she heard Seth's voice.

"Charlotte! Mrs. Garrity!" He hurried toward them in the passageway.

Despite the fact that he had addressed her by her proper name, Charlotte began to close her door on him, but he wedged it open with his shoulder. "Charlotte, I'm sorry for what I said. Will you please forgive me?"

She pushed hard against the door, but couldn't make it shut. "Go away, Seth!"

He struggled against her weight, keeping the door from latching. "I promise . . . I'll never call you 'Charlie' again. Say you'll . . . forgive me. If Mrs. Garrity says it's all right, I want to take you to the Fair on my day off." He turned to the teacher, still battling to keep the door from closing. "May I please have . . . your permission?"

From behind her door, Charlotte pleaded, her voice sounding strained from her effort to keep Seth at bay. "Mrs. Garrity . . . don't listen to him. Tell him to go away. I don't want . . . anything to do with him!"

"Charlotte, why didn't you ever tell me you had such a delightful nickname?" Mrs. Garrity asked. "Charlie fits you perfectly. I love it!"

At her teacher's words, Charlotte let her door slam open. Seth fell in a heap at her feet. She stepped over him, into the passageway. "Did I hear you right, Mrs. Garrity? Did you say you *like* the name Charlie?"

Her teacher was grinning broadly. "It's perfectly charming! But if you prefer, I'll continue to call you Charlotte."

She thought for several moments. Her gaze shifted from her teacher, to Seth, now standing beside her. "You both may call me Charlie," she said solemnly. Turning to her teacher, she continued. "Mrs. Garrity, with your permission, I would like very much for Seth to come with us to the Fair on his day off."

"Permission granted."

Seth breathed a sigh of relief. "Thank you, Mrs. Garrity! Thank you! I'll see you later." He gave a slight bow and trotted off, bringing a smile of amusement to Helen Garrity's face when she turned to her pupil.

"I'll see you at dinner . . . "

Helen let herself in her room and began the task of unpacking. From habit, she stored her undergarments in the left side of the built-in mahogany dresser. The empty right side made her more than a bit lonesome for Robert.

Until her trip to South Manitou Island last fall, they had always occupied this cabin and this drawer together. She thought she would be able to control her grief, but a lump formed stubbornly in her throat as she glanced up at his framed sketch of the high school in Ann Arbor where she had once taught. In another frame beside it, was a rendering of University Hall in the same town, where he had spent so much of his time. Her eyes grew misty thinking of the happiness they had shared until Robert's illness had intervened, reducing him to an invalid, and eventually stealing him from her.

Perhaps she shouldn't have agreed to come on this trip. Martha had already proved herself as irascible as ever. She would have to have grace in abundance to keep from telling the opinionated woman off before this trip came to an end.

Then there was George. Beneath that pompous, gruff, cigar-smoking exterior lay a good-hearted man, but would he ever let up on his hard-driving business pursuits long enough to peel off the outer layers and expose the soft, sentimental soul beneath?

After Charlotte had put all of her belongings away in the beautiful dresser drawers lined with hyacinth-scented paper, she took out the tiny sewing kit Aurora had insisted she bring along, and mended the tear in her skirt. Aurora must have known she would need needle and thread before her trip was over.

Soon enough, dinner hour was upon her and she made her way to the main saloon, somehow managing to endure the evening meal, with its cold tomato soup appetizer, broiled trout fish course, hearty prime rib main course with boiled potatoes smothered in cheese sauce, buttered spring peas, and fresh blueberry flummery for dessert. Eating seemed to be an important pastime of the well-to-do. So far as she could tell, Martha Garrity divided her time among such limited pursuits as reading, eating, and being generally disagreeable. Charlotte hadn't expected such irritable and irritating company on the trip, and she had to keep constant guard over her tongue to refrain from speaking her mind. Martha was the slowest eater and most verbose conversationalist Charlotte had ever known.

After dinner, George withdrew outside where his cigar smoke wouldn't bother "his ladies," as he put it. Meanwhile, Charlotte's teacher engaged Martha in conversation. In a remarkably short time, the elder Mrs. Garrity managed to express her disapproval of everyone in the world of Christendom who was neither Protestant, Republican, nor wealthy. Evidently a few minutes of prickly remarks was enough for Helen. She soon followed George to the afterdeck, leaving Charlotte to hold her own with the difficult woman.

George was sprawled in one of the wicker chairs which he had positioned near enough to the port rail to extend his arm and flick off burnt ash from his cigar into the lake when necessary. Helen buttoned her suit jacket against the cool evening air and drew up a chair beside him, upwind of his smoke.

When he saw her, his gray eyes lit up. "I didn't expect to see you out in this cold, foul air," he quipped.

"It's not terribly cold, and it will cease being foul the moment you've tossed out your cigar. But don't let me ruin your after-dinner smoke," she said facetiously.

"Too late." He took one last drag, threw away the half-smoked cigar, then sat more erect. "I can't tell you how wonderful it is to have you aboard, Helen." His tone was ambiguous, and from the smirk on his face, he knew it.

"Give me the truth, George. Are you really glad to see me, or has my obvious distaste for smoking caused an imposition? To be perfectly honest, I don't see how your mother has put up with it all these years."

"You know Mother. In her mind, I can do no wrong. I'm sure she takes pity on me, since I've never found a woman who could convince me to marry." He gave a laugh, reaching for her hand, but she snatched it away.

"George, you know I don't like public displays of affection," she reminded him.

"It's your own fault," he teased, "I'm just trying to reply to your question as to whether or not I'm glad to see you. Since you won't allow me to *show* you the answer, I suppose I shall simply have to tell you that I'm pleased to have you aboard. Now, since we're in the mood for honesty, you tell me. Are you glad to see me, or do you just put up with me because I'm a free ride to the Fair?"

CHAPTER 7

"I am both glad to see you, and pleased to have free passage to the Fair," she answered honestly. "I do wish you'd find yourself a wife to supply your need for affection, though."

"A wife? Botheration! I've heard it said wives are not the most reliable source of affection, at least not where some husbands are concerned."

"George Garrity! You should be ashamed of yourself, leveling such a criticism at married women!"

George chuckled. "I'm certain my philosophy comes as no shock to you. After all, we've known one another for—what is it? Eight years now? Besides, you know I'm only referring to *some* women."

"Which means others would make perfectly suitable

wives," she concluded.

"Sounds good in theory, but in practice, things don't work out quite so easily. Despite what you may think, I've been looking for a wife for years, and I've discovered that all the women worth marrying are already taken, leaving me to steal affection where I can. As you've noticed, I'm a willing recipient of cast-off kisses the likes of yours."

"Which really leads me to wonder—"

"Wonder what, my dear?"

"How I'm going to convince you to switch to a different topic."

"Such as?"

"The new fellow you hired on."

"Now, Helen, don't you think he's a bit young for you?"

"George Garrity! You can be absolutely infuriating at times!"

He grinned broadly. "I pride myself on it."

"Now pride yourself on being serious for a moment."

"If you insist, but let me warn you, it will be difficult. Now, what about this boy—Seth, is it? He hasn't caused trouble already, has he? It's usually Mother who's complaining about the crew."

"No trouble. It's just that he's asked whether he can spend his day off with Charlotte and me at the Fair. I've given my permission. I just wanted you to know."

His gray eyes lit with a gleam. "How about making your threesome into a foursome and letting me treat the lot of you to a real frolic on the Midway?"

"Frolic? You? I didn't think you could put aside your business affairs long enough to take a day off for pleasure."

"Watch me!" he challenged. "Let's plan it for Monday.

By then, you and your friend will have had your fill of the exhibitions on the grounds proper. It will be our last fling before we leave Jackson Park."

Helen had a thought that put a wrinkle between her brows. "Do you suppose Martha will want to join us at the Fair on Monday?"

He threw his head back and let out a loud guffaw. "Great guns, no! She's planning to spend her time with her sister, my Aunt Mercy, on Lakeshore Drive. I doubt the two of them will spend more than a day in Jackson Park. I've already heard Mother say if she goes to the Fair at all, she most certainly will *not* step foot on the Midway. It's really quite a carnival there, you know."

"So I've read," Helen responded dryly.

"Don't sound so skeptical. Trust me. You'll enjoy the change. I guarantee it to be a jolly good time."

"If you say so, George." She remained unconvinced.

While Mrs. Garrity spoke with George on the afterdeck, Charlotte sat on the blue velvet sofa, listening as patiently as she could to Martha run on about her friends in Detroit.

"The Morgan Fenwicks are high up in banking. I dare say old Morgan owns a goodly share of National Bank stock. Then there are the Beardsleys. They manufacture fine furniture. They produced all of the mahogany and oak pieces on this yacht. They've even made furniture for President Cleveland.

"The Pingrees are known far and wide for their shoes. Earned a fortune at it, too. Every year old H.S. buys his wife a huge new diamond for her birthday.

"But of course, I'm most impressed with George and the success he's made of himself in the stove business. He started with nothing, and now he owns the second largest stove works in Detroit.

"City life is the only life for me. Have you ever been to Detroit, Miss Richards?"

"No, ma'am. I haven't."

"No? What cities have you visited?"

Charlotte thought a moment. "I was in Kalamazoo once when I was really small. I don't remember much about it, though."

"Kalamazoo?" The old woman said it with obvious disdain.

"Yes, ma'am."

"Not much of a town. I'm afraid I just can't abide small cities or small towns. They're so . . . *bucolic*, what with chickens running loose and cows tied in the side yard. Some folks even raise pigs in town. Can you imagine? I never could understand it. If they wanted to raise livestock, they should have bought a place in the country and taken up farming." Martha put her nose in the air and glanced out the window before turning again to Charlotte.

"To tell you the truth, I don't see how you manage on that pitiful little island of yours. It must be pretty dull company you keep. Not much going on there, I conjecture. You have no manufacturing facilities, no department stores, no theater, no literary club, no concert hall—none of the amenities that make life worth living. Why, that small patch of land could sink right to the bottom of the lake, and who would miss it?"

Charlotte's blood began to boil. "Begging your pardon, ma'am, but South Manitou Island is very important to folks out on the lakes. It's the only harbor of refuge between the Straits of Mackinac and Chicago. Captains steer by the light on our tower. If it weren't for the lighthouse and us lightkeepers, a lot of boats wouldn't be able to make it through the Manitou Passage. You're wrong to criticize people and places you don't understand. In fact, everything you've said today about South Manitou shows how *little* you know about it!"

Martha's cheeks blossomed with bright red patches. "You impudent child! Were it not for your friendship with Helen, I'd see to it you were put off at Chicago and sent directly home by the most expedient means available!"

Charlotte jumped up from the sofa. "Go ahead. Put me off. I won't mind a bit. I thought it was supposed to be a real treat riding on a yacht to Chicago. So far, it hasn't been very pleasant at all. I'd have more fun rowing the light service boat!" She ran out, bumping headlong into Helen in the doorway.

Her teacher caught her by the shoulders. "Charlie, what's wrong?"

"I'm sorry, Mrs. Garrity! Really, I am! But I just couldn't take it anymore!" Charlotte broke free, traveling through the passageway to her cabin at a near run.

"What's gotten into her?" George wondered.

Helen's glance darted to her mother-in-law, then back to George. "I'll go find out."

The corner of his mouth curled and he bent to whisper in Helen's ear. "Mother's been practicing her own brand of congeniality, no doubt."

Helen spoke softly. "Why don't you try to make sense of your mother's side of things?"

He nodded. "Some days, it's not easy being Martha Garrity's son."

Hot tears streamed down Charlotte's face as she yanked open her dresser drawer, lifted the bag she had unpacked a short while ago onto the luggage rack, and began tossing in handkerchiefs, chemises, petticoats and underdrawers. A quiet tapping on her door, accompanied by the sound of her teacher's voice, gave her pause. She grabbed one of the handkerchiefs from her bag and carelessly dried her eyes before opening the door.

"Won't you tell me what's wrong, Charlie?" her teacher quietly asked.

Charlotte motioned for her to come inside, retrieved a second handkerchief from her bag and blew her nose before answering. "I'm just not meant to get along with that lady. I'm going home!" she said through her tears.

"Surely you don't mean that."

"Yes, I do! She doesn't want me around, and I couldn't possibly keep from arguing with her for a whole week!"

"But what about the Fair? What about me? I want you around!"

"You and your mother-in-law will have more fun at the Fair without me. Seth was right. You never should have invited me. I'm just an ordinary island girl. I don't know how to get along with folks like your mother-in-law. I'm nothing but trouble."

"Oh, Charlie, don't say that. It isn't true!"

"But it is! Since I got on this boat, I've ripped my new skirt on the machinery in the engine room," she pulled up the hem showing her mending, "nearly gotten Seth dismissed in the process, and made your mother-in-law so angry she says she'd put me off the boat if it weren't for my friendship with you. I don't want to cause any more trouble, and I don't want to be around *her*. Don't you see?

I *have* to go back to the island."

"Running away isn't the answer to your problems," Helen said calmly, putting an arm about Charlotte's shoulders. "You can't always avoid people who are difficult to get along with. Sometimes you have to look for a way to smooth troubled waters."

Charlotte dabbed her eyes and looked up. "But how would I do that?"

"The first thing you have to do is understand that you can't change someone else, and accept them the way they are. It helps to know that sometimes they behave the way they do because they lack confidence in themselves."

Charlotte thought for a moment. "But your mother-in-law is about the boldest person I ever met. She just spent half an hour bragging about all the important people she knows in Detroit!"

"That's her outward appearance. Inside, she's unsure of herself. She's not quite certain people respect her. That's why she carries on so. When you're with her, you have to be a good listener, try not to contradict her even when you don't agree, and occasionally pay her a compliment. Then things will go a lot more smoothly between you."

"I don't know if it will work. I don't think I can keep my temper under control when I'm around her."

"You can if you really want to. And I hope you'll want to, because I'm not letting you go back to South Manitou Island until the *Martha G.* does." She gave Charlotte a hug, then set her at arm's length, hands on her shoulders. "You've only got tonight and tomorrow at breakfast to exercise control over your temper. After that, Mother Garrity is going to her sister's on Lakeshore Drive and we won't see her again until it's time to sail home."

A great burden lifted from Charlotte's heart, and she suddenly felt light as the fluffy clouds she often saw floating above her island home. "I thought every day would be spent with her. Maybe you're right. Maybe I *could* manage until tomorrow . . . I'm *sure* I can."

"I'm sure you can, too. Now put your things away. If you feel up to it, come out to the lounge." She started to go, then turned back to add, "And Charlie, don't go near the engine room again. I don't imagine Stokes was too pleased to see a young lady in his lair, and I'm certain George would be most upset if he knew."

"I won't go there ever again, Mrs. Garrity. I promise!"

When she awoke the following morning on the *Martha G.*, at anchor in the outer harbor at Jackson Park, Charlotte could hardly believe the shoreline scene visible from her cabin window. She had read of the White City, but had never imagined anything quite so grand as the pristine classical structures that stood along and behind the water's edge. Mrs. Garrity had said that the Manufactures and Liberal Arts Building was one of the largest, and Charlotte had no trouble picking it out, with its long array of two-storied columns and fluted archways. She had also learned of criticisms of its design, but couldn't imagine anyone being disappointed in such a grand façade.

Closer to the water and just left of the grandiose structure stood the Peristyle, and from it the long, wide steamboat pier stretched out into the harbor. Flanking the Manufactures Building on the opposite end rose the U.S. Government Building, with its capitol-like dome and the flag atop rising high into the sky for all to see.

Somewhere in the background behind the larger exposition halls lay the Woman's Building of which Mrs. Garrity had often spoken. Charlotte had seen drawings of the Italian Renaissance design by Sophia Hayden, winner of the architectural competition, and could hardly wait to visit it.

But dominating the skyline, visible though a great distance back from the water, stood the most incredible feat of engineering ever erected at any fair—George Washington Gale Ferris's two hundred sixty-four-foot wheel! This, more than anything else, made Charlotte believe she had actually arrived at the Fair. She simply sat on her bed and stared at it in wonder, thinking how grand must be the view from the top.

After awhile, her imaginings gave way to the realization she had only fifteen minutes to wash and dress for breakfast, or Martha would refuse her a place at the breakfast table. She quickly laid out her skirt and waist, stockings and shoes, then went to her sink to wash up. My, how convenient to have both hot and cold running water. It made her usual accommodations at the keeper's quarters on South Manitou seem primitive, indeed.

At breakfast, she kept tight control of her tongue, exchanging morning greetings in a pleasant manner, speaking only when spoken to, responding in the most polite method she could manage. The variety and amount of food offered at the sideboard truly astounded her—hot biscuits, gravy, sausage and bacon, sweet rolls, muffins, a chafing dish full of scrambled eggs and cheese, plenty of hot coffee for the adults and another carafe of hot chocolate all to herself. Everything she tried tasted so wonderful, she ate until she was uncomfortably full, then took herself on a walk about the deck in the fresh air, longing for departure to the dock.

Half an hour later, George ordered his navigator to lift the anchor and make way for the Fifty-Sixth Street pier, bragging that he had made special arrangements with the Columbian Navigation Company, who had exclusive use of the dock, for disembarking from the *Martha G.* Charlotte was on the foredeck with her teacher, watching their approach while George rattled on.

"Now, ladies, I have something important to say to you before we go off to the Exposition." From his breast pocket he pulled out a folded paper and opened it up, holding it against the deck rail in the fluttering breeze. "Here's a map of the grounds. We'll get off this dock and enter here." He indicated the points with his index finger. "It's a short two-block walk from the pier and will bring us in pretty close to the Woman's Building." He followed a walking route with his little finger. "I assume that will be our first destination."

Helen grinned. "How thoughtful of you, George!"

He simply winked, then folded the map and handed it to her before taking a duplicate from his pocket. He offered it to Charlotte, leveling his gaze on her. "Miss Richards, if you stay with Helen and me at all times like you're supposed to, you won't even need this map, but I want you to have one, just in case. If we get separated, go to the entrance I showed you and wait."

"Thank you, sir. I'll do that," she solemnly promised, shoving the map into her skirt pocket.

"At five o'clock, the pilot will meet us at the same place on the dock where he leaves us off," George explained. Reaching deep into his pants pocket, he came up with some change. He picked out two silver dollars and offered them to Charlotte. "These are for you, young lady, for when you find a few mementos you'd like to take home."

She hesitated. He had already been wonderfully generous. Besides, the five dollar gold piece her mother had provided was knotted into her handkerchief and pinned securely inside her skirt pocket. "I . . . "

"Go on. Take it," George said almost gruffly.

With an approving nod from her teacher, she accepted the gift. "I don't know what to say, except thank you."

"Just don't spend it all in one place," George advised. "Now if you'll excuse me, ladies, I'd better get up to the bridge. We're about to dock."

Within moments, George's deck hand had put out the gangway. George helped Helen and Charlotte from the slightly tipsy boat onto the dock, then assisted as his crew cast off again, eager to get out of the way of the Columbian Navigation Company's steamer arriving with its first load of passengers for the day.

"If we move quickly, we'll beat the crowd that's about to disembark from that boat," George suggested, taking Helen and Charlotte each by the elbow. Within minutes they had reached the Exposition. George's prior purchase of tickets allowed them to bypass the long lines at the ticket booths and proceed directly to the turnstyle. Charlotte deposited her ticket and pressed on the bar for admittance.

The moment she stepped foot on the fairgrounds, she was awestruck by the magnificence of the place. Everywhere she looked, classical architecture filled her view. Momentarily, she was dazed by the forest of buildings.

"We'll pass several state expositions on our way to the Woman's Building," George explained. "On our left is the Texas Building."

"It certainly is attractive. I like its Spanish design," Helen observed.

With so much impressive architecture, Charlotte found it a challenge to focus on one building at a time, but the Texas exhibit was an imposing sight. Its twin towers flying the American and Lone Star flags above grounds planted in native tropical foliage of banana, palm, magnolia, pomegranate, Spanish dagger, and orange.

In front of them, the great pillared porch of a Kentucky plantation stretched in welcome, and beyond that, the North Dakotan colonial design of a two-story-high columned porch. Farther on, the Arkansas Building to their left resembled the ornate French rococo style, including its elliptical veranda.

"Look to your right," Mrs. Garrity suggested. "There's Nebraska's version of a colonial design. I like the large portico on each side of the building."

"And over there is the Minnesota building." George pointed across the way. "It has a roof of metallic Spanish tiles. And guess whose statues are standing on the portico, Miss Richards?"

As Charlotte drew near, she began to make them out. "It looks like an Indian couple, but who?"

"I'll give you a hint," said her teacher. "They were made famous by a poem Longfellow wrote."

"Then the man must be Hiawatha," she concluded.

Mrs. Garrity nodded. "And the woman is Minnehaha."

Next on the right, they passed South Dakota's two-story edifice with arched windows and a portico across the front. Beyond it, Washington state had erected their exposition building entirely of lumber, celebrating their most important industry.

Also on the right stood Colorado's two slender towers in a style reminiscent of Spanish Renaissance, and across from it the Michigan building.

The Michigan State Building.

"Our home state has made a respectable showing for itself," Mrs. Garrity concluded. "I like the tall tower."

"Three stories," George pointed out.

"And I like the huge veranda that goes all the way across the front, and the balcony and windows on the tower," Charlotte commented.

George pointed to the opposite side of the way. "California has reproduced a mission. It's too plain, for my taste."

Turning in the opposite direction, Helen caught her breath. "You certainly can't say that about Wisconsin's style. Just look at it! A brownstone base, red brick for the first floor, a shingled upper story—and those brownstone pillars and granite columns supporting its porch certainly give it substance."

The Wisconsin State Building.

Beyond the Wisconsin building Charlotte saw something entirely different. "Mrs. Garrity, what style is the Indiana building? I've never seen anything like it!"

"That's called Gothic, Charlie. Isn't it beautiful? It has

some wonderful elements for its period—cathedral windows, turrets, towers, and tall spires at each end rising high above the roof. They did nice work of finishing the first story in Indiana graystone, and the upper two in wood."

They passed the Indiana building, a public comfort station and bicycle court before they came to the north end of a larger structure.

George stopped in the walkway. "There it is. The Woman's Building."

"The result of much planning by Mrs. Palmer and her Board of Lady Managers," Helen said in awe.

Charlotte was struck by the beauty of the building. Despite all that she had heard and read about it in school, she hadn't expected so impressive a structure.

"Let's go around to the front, shall we?" George suggested. "You'll want to experience the full effect of the façade before we go inside."

CHAPTER 8

The eastern exposure of the Woman's Building, which faced a lagoon, offered a triple arched entrance at its center, flanked by walls with double pilasters. Stretching to each end, the first story had been fashioned in the form of an Italian arcade surrounded with a portico roof which served as a balcony for the second story. Above this was an open colonnade with a pediment richly decorated in bas-relief.

"It's amazing to me that this whole building was paid for by women," Charlotte said in wonder.

"I don't believe it," George stated flatly.

Helen leveled her gaze on him. "Don't tease now,

George. You know very well it's true."

"And where do you suppose those women got the money they contributed for it?" he asked sardonically. "From their husbands, their fathers, or estates left by men. It's a known fact most women depend upon men for their economic survival, so it's men who built this building," he neatly concluded.

Helen knew George was baiting her, and she felt her anger rising. "Men may have raised the girders and plastered the walls, but there would have been no labor for them without the money women collected for the purpose, no matter what its source," she firmly countered. "Now I suggest we put that issue to rest before we confuse Charlie, and go inside."

Charlotte felt a special thrill as she stepped into the central hall. It opened onto a sizable rotunda that featured a skylight, giving the feeling of vastness and open spaces that easily accommodated the large artistic renderings decorating its interior.

"There's Mrs. MacMonnies' mural of primitive woman," Helen pointed out, indicating the artwork beneath the name *Bertha H. Palmer* on the north tympanum.

"I suppose the collection of females in that artwork has special meaning," George said a trifle cynically.

"Of course!" Charlie replied, undaunted by his attitude. "In school, we learned that the central figure represents motherhood."

"Then who are those females on either side, sowing seed and carrying jars of water?" he challenged.

Charlotte couldn't remember any discussion about those figures in the painting, but she turned her smile on him and stated confidently, "Her daughters, naturally."

George rolled his eyes upward. "Naturally."

Charlotte nearly chuckled at the ingenuity of her made-up answer as she studied the work a few moments longer. Turning to the contrasting piece on the opposite wall beneath the name of *Sophia G. Hayden*, she recognized the origin of the work immediately. "That must be the mural by Mary Cassatt," she concluded.

"You remembered!" Helen exclaimed. "I had wondered whether anyone had paid attention the day I told the class about it."

Charlotte studied the piece entitled "Modern Woman" depicting a group of young girls in pursuit of a figure of flame which was disappearing in the distant blue heavens, expecting George to make a critical remark about it at any moment, but he turned his attention to the rotunda instead.

"Just look at these display cases. Row after row of them filled with needlework and ivory painting. There must be something about them we men can take credit for."

"Building the frames and putting in the glass, I would guess," Helen concluded wryly.

He moved on to the central fountain bordered with aquatic plants, and a sculpture consisting of a cluster of figures. "The women who decorated this place must have stolen this statuary from some park over in Europe."

"How can you say such a thing?" Helen asked indignantly. "You know the work was commissioned specifically for this building—figures of Psyche, Maud Müller, and busts of C.B. Winslow, Susan B. Anthony, and Elizabeth Cady Stanton."

George scratched his bearded chin. "Well, so they are."

"That's right, Mr. Garrity," Charlotte put in. "They represent women who help to make the world a better place."

"Miss Richards, you're mighty smart for a young lady of . . . thirteen? I can tell it's going to be tough to pull the wool over your eyes," George acknowledged.

Helen led them toward the east side of the rotunda. "If you two don't mind, I'd like to take a look at the Educational Room now."

George had only to step past the threshold into the roomful of showcases to know that Helen would want to spend far more time here than would he. "Ladies, if you'll excuse me, I think I'll step outside to indulge my nasty cigar habit. I'd better check on my stove display over at the Manufactures Building, too. I'll be back after a spell."

Though Helen had in mind to suggest he give up smoking, thus eliminating his need for escape, she thought better of it. "You take your time, George. I'm sure we'll be here for a good long while."

As Charlotte moved with her teacher through the room filled with wall hangings, framed prints, and displays, she couldn't help but admire the work of each of the many talented women. Architectural drawings, designs for carpets, book covers, wallpaper, oil cloth and printed textiles all came from New York institutions such as the School of Applied Designs for Women, the School of Industrial Art, and the Pratt Institute. The Pennsylvania College for Women provided displays concerning women in medicine, as did nurses training schools in New York and Philadelphia. Even the American School for Girls at Scutari, Turkey, had submitted a display of drawings and needlework.

When they had seen their fill, they wandered into the adjoining section where an eclectic display traced industries of women. There, they found a large Pennsylvania sheep, indicative of the shearing industry which employed thousands of the nation's women. Raw silks and silken fabrics filled a glass case, evidence of skilled women in Utah and several other states engaged in raising cocoons. Another display featured portable kilns patented by women, pottery items, and hand-knitted woolen goods from Iceland.

George was waiting outside the Education Room when Charlotte and her teacher finished there. The odor of cigar smoke clinging to his jacket put Charlotte off. "You know, Mr. Garrity, you really ought to quit smoking. You missed a lot of interesting things in the Education Room. Besides, those cigars of yours don't make you smell very good."

George put a hand on his hip. "Miss Richards, are you telling me I stink?" he asked a bit gruffly.

The way he spoke reminded her of her father when he was teasing. "That's exactly what I mean," she said, grinning.

"That's some thanks I get for bringing you to the Fair today."

Helen took a step closer, testing the air. "She's right, George. Your coat smells like it was salvaged from a cigar factory fire, as usual."

"Just maybe I should have left the both of you on South Manitou Island," he grumbled.

"You can't blame Charlie for speaking up about it. Hardly anyone on the island ever lights a cigar."

George harrumphed. "Don't know what they're missing."

"And thank goodness for that," Helen added. "Now, since we're likely to find no solution to the cigar problem, shall we get on with our tour?"

Charlotte pointed to the west side of the hall. "Mr. Garrity, what do you suppose they've put in the Scientific Rooms?"

"Blamed if I know. Let's find out."

They hadn't been in the room long when Mrs. Garrity made an interesting discovery. "George, Charlie, look at this. *Notes on the Satellites of Saturn* by Maria Mitchell, late professor of Vassar College."

George perused the item with a jaundiced eye. "What could some teacher at a woman's college possibly know about that subject?" he challenged.

"Evidently enough to write an entire volume on it that deserved to be published," Helen quipped. "It's proof women can accomplish anything they set their minds to, whether you want to admit it or not."

George backed away. "All right, so the woman knows her astronomy. She's got to be one in a million. Now let's see what else is in this room."

He led Helen and Charlotte to a display of maps and drawings by women in the employ of the Surveyor-General's Office, admitting they showed remarkable skill and talent. Adjacent were mineral, fossil, and botanical specimens from women around the world.

From there, they wandered through the main hallway of the northern wing, pausing to admire the doll-like dummies dressed in various costumes on loan from the women of New York, depicting the evolution of American History. Among them were a Spanish woman of St. Augustine in full skirt and lace mantilla, a colonial maiden of New Amsterdam, a Puritan, a Quakeress, a New York woman elegantly attired in silks and furs, a matron of Revolutionary times, a hoop-skirted figure of the Civil War era, and fashionable women of the present day, dressed in the latest Parisian styles.

George lingered by one of the contemporary mannequins. "You'd look wonderful in something like this, Helen," he commented, fingering the ruffled lace that overlaid the shoulder of the black silk jacket.

"Nonsense," she argued. "I'd have no place to wear it. Besides, Worth creations cost a fortune."

"You know what's the trouble with you, Helen? You're too practical!"

"That's a fault I can neither deny, nor regret," she admitted. "Now, shall we move on?"

They perused a large central display by ladies of Spain and Spanish-America. Women had gone to great lengths to present a beautiful and thorough collection of their artistic talent and industry. Specimens of their handicrafts included needlework, knitting, crocheting, lacemaking, handloomed pieces, embroidery, tapestries, embossing, domestic cloths both fine and coarse, and other textiles indigenous to various regions. Other displays recognized women's labor in the tobacco industry, for which George heartily expressed his approval. Several choice examples of fabrics represented the work of deaf and dumb women.

Next came items from the Orient. Japan had sent a unique representation of a boudoir of a Feudal Lord's wife of olden times including items of the toilet. A library display featured stringed instruments, mats, screens, banners, books, and other furnishings. Aside from these, the Japanese had sent oil paintings, ivory carvings, cocoons, raw silk embroideries, crinkled textures and crepes, tapestries, laces, cloissonne, enamel work, porcelain dinnerware, lacquer work, and artificial flowers.

From the Royal House of Savoy was a display of handmade laces in intricate patterns of flowers and leaves against delicate mesh backgrounds. The French showed their own laces such as D'Alencon, Chantilly and French pointlaces, as well as trousseaus for matrons, young girls, and infants.

Mexico presented a tasteful arrangement of fancywork including artificial fruits and flowers. Among articles in the tea-house-like display of Ceylon were carved tables, light draperies, and dainty cups of wood. Brazil showed samples of fancywork done in feathers and fish scales, while Belgium offered embroideries, laces, and water colors by the queen. The Archduchess Maria Theresa of Austria sent a screen she had painted, and Germany produced decorated china and leather executed by women who had received instruction in the industrial schools of her empire.

From the south portion of the first floor, George escorted Charlotte and Helen to the organization department where industrial, educational, religious, and other associations of women had set up headquarters. The largest was the Woman's Christian Temperance Union, with more than two hundred thousand active members. Another impressive organization was the Women's Educational and Industrial Association which included seventeen unions.

George insisted next on visiting the model kitchen. Charlotte understood his interest when he pointed out the modern gas cookstove. "No wood to chop, no fire to light and keep fed. What would your mother think if she had something like this in the keeper's quarters?"

"It sure would be a convenience," Charlotte admitted. "But how would she get the gas to run it?"

"It will be a few years before gas is common on South Manitou," he conceded, "but the day will come when appliances the likes of these replace the wood-burning stoves, and stove works like mine will have to change, or go out of business."

"Do you really think so, George, with all the wood on the island?"

"That timber won't last forever."

"I suppose not, but I just can't imagine giving up the warmth and coziness of a well-tended cookstove."

Upon leaving the model kitchen, Charlotte found herself drawn toward the library. Helen and George followed, stopping just outside the door.

"If you ladies don't mind, I'll leave you to see the rest of this building on your own. I need to check on my stove display in the Manufactures Building. Shall we meet outside the east entrance in an hour?"

Helen checked the watch hanging from her pin. "Noon outside the east entrance."

"Bring an appetite," he added, then strode toward the exit.

When he was out of earshot, Charlotte added, "Don't bring a cigar."

"That's one habit I don't have any real hope of changing in George," Helen admitted ruefully. "Shall we see what we can find in the library now?"

The room contained seven thousand volumes, all written by women, as well as autographs and portraits of women from France, Great Britain, and America.

When they had finished in the library, they visited the Keppel Collection, an intriguing array of work by women engravers dating back to 1581, and the work of Diana Ghisi of Mantua, who had engraved plates with copies of works from Raphael, Tuccari, and Guilio Romano. French, Italian, German, and English women were also represented among the specimens that dated from 1535 to 1835.

The next exhibit Charlotte visited with her teacher was that of the British training schools for nurses. Beneath a portrait of Queen Victoria stood a statue of Florence Nightingale. Glass cases exhibited ligatures and bandages, thermometers, surgical dressings, and the like. Another display showed the uniforms, lacy caps, and badges worn by those in the nursing profession.

Adjoining this exhibit, Charlotte admired jewelry on display by New York women of West African descent, cabinets decorated by a wood-burning technique, as well as fancywork and bookbinding done by dark-skinned ladies.

Their tour continued, past embroideries of Russia and Rumania, Fayal and Ceylon, Greece and Arabia, South America and Mexico, and those of the Orient. So fascinated had Charlotte been that she hadn't realized how much time had passed until her stomach rumbled, making her realize it must be nearly midday.

"What do you say we go meet George?" Helen suggested. "After lunch, we could visit the Children's Building, if you'd like."

"That sounds like a good plan."

George was waiting when they stepped outside onto the portico that faced the lagoon. The bright sunshine made Charlotte squint. She stood a moment, getting her bearings. "I've seen so much, my mind is in a fog. I feel dazed by it all."

"You've only just begun your week at the Fair. I hope you're not tired of it already," George said.

"Goodness, no!" Charlotte assured him. "I'm just ready for a rest and something good to eat."

"Then I've got just the place. We'll go to the Swedish Restaurant." George held out an arm for each of the ladies.

When Helen tucked her hand in his elbow, she noticed how much the smoke smell had faded. Was it possible he hadn't indulged a cigar since mid-morning?

George led them toward the water's edge where a gondola slid past. It was propelled by two gondoliers in bright-colored costumes reminiscent of the fourteenth century. Long feathers jutted rakishly from their little caps. And they were wearing crimson velvet tunics with gathered silk sleeves that poufed at the shoulders and elbows. Sash belts dripping with fringe were tied off to the side, and on their legs were striped knee-length pants that met long stockings much like a ballet dancer's tights. To George, they looked silly in all that get-up, but they seemed to be doing a regular enough business. He supposed that sort of thing held much appeal for the gentler sex. Glancing at

Gondolier.

Helen, he wondered whether she would enjoy such a ride after lunch. He supposed they'd have to have the kid along, too.

He noticed Helen pressing a hand to the small of her back. He remembered now that she had suffered from backaches in the days of her marriage to Robert. A gondola ride would be just the cure. But how to get shed of the ace girl student?

He puzzled that one over while taking the path past the Illinois Building, a Greek cross configuration with a huge dome rising from the center. Following the path to the eastern side of the Fair, they passed the Merchant Tailors' Building, a Greek Revival affair with six pillars in front which added stature to what would otherwise be dwarfed by the size of its neighbor.

Here, a foot bridge took them over the waterway that connected the lagoon with the North Pond, and they continued past the Japanese Tea House, built in the traditional style of *kinoti*—two structures, actually—of wood and bamboo, with tiles on the roofs.

Finally they arrived at their destination, designed after a tavern in Southern Sweden. The line of hungry patrons waiting for a table was not long, and shortly they were seated in the dim interior at a highly polished pine table and presented with menus.

"It's pretty dark for reading a menu," Charlotte observed, straining to make out the list of offerings.

"I can tell you what it says," George volunteered. "Smoked reindeer, baby sausages, crawfish tails, raw *delikatess*, herring, fried stromming, smoked goose breast, reindeer tongue, and *graflax*."

Charlotte lowered her menu. "Mr. Garrity, what on

earth is *graflax*?"

"I'm not really sure, but I tried it here soon after the restaurant opened, and I don't think anyone but a Swede could eat it. It forced me into taking a shot of *brannvin* to wash it down."

"*Brannvin?*" Helen asked.

"Potato whiskey. I rarely touch spirits, but I had to dilute whatever it was they had put in the *graflax*."

"Did it work?" Charlotte wanted to know.

"Must have. I don't remember getting sick," he concluded.

Charlotte perused the American side of the menu, quickly locating an item suitable to her taste. "I'm getting the open-face roast beef sandwich. What are you going to order, Mrs. Garrity?"

"I think I'll order the Swedish sampler, a taste of any five native offerings. I doubt I'll see the likes of this menu again anytime soon. I might as well take advantage while I'm here."

Their server promptly appeared to take their orders and serve beverages, and though every table in the eatery was buzzing with conversation, the service was efficient and the atmosphere conducive to a most pleasant repast—except for Charlotte's one daring venture into foreign cuisine when she tried a bite of Helen's reindeer tongue. She quickly downed the last of her milk, and ordered a Swedish pastry filled with cream to banish the lingering aftertaste.

When they had finished, George paid the check, threw a dollar on the table for a tip, earning him a skeptical look from Charlotte, then escorted the women outdoors into the bright sunshine. Out of habit, he reached for the fat cigar in his inside breast pocket, but left it there. He had the blamedest urge to light it up, but thought better of it, considering the response he was likely to get from his two lady friends.

"George," Helen turned her pretty blue eyes on him. "I promised Charlotte she could see the Children's Building after lunch. Would that suit you?"

Aware of the activities there that would occupy the little student while he and Helen slipped away on a gondola, he bowed gallantly. "Most certainly."

CHAPTER 9

George silently formulated his plan for whisking Helen off alone as he approached the Children's Building. There, a center court offered a sunny play area, while its rooftop playground was safely enclosed by railing and netting.

"The first thing I want to do is show Miss Richards the woodworking that is done by young people in a specially equipped facility called the sloyd room. I think she could make some very useful item there that would serve as a memento of her trip," he said, opening the door in the arched entryway. He referred to the workshop that had been designed to teach children the use of hand tools. He had learned of it weeks ago, before the Fair opened, and wanted to see for himself how it operated.

Moments later, they stepped into a room with tall windows that provided bright, natural light for the displays, charts, and other learning aids posted on the walls. It also contained a series of workbenches, each equipped with a vise, a rack of tools, and a stool. Two young fellows and a young lady approximately Charlotte's age were already busy at their work stations fashioning wooden items under the watchful eye of a supervisor. A dark-haired fellow of medium height and wearing thick glasses, he appeared to be a year or two older than Seth. When he saw George and the ladies enter, he came to greet them.

"Welcome. I'm Mr. Underhill."

George pumped the younger man's hand, then he pressed his palm against Charlotte's back, pushing her forward. "I have a young lady here, Miss Richards, who would like some instruction in sloyd. Do you think you could help her out?"

"I'd be glad to. Right this way, Miss Richards."

The three of them followed Mr. Underhill to an unoccupied workbench where he took up a blank piece of pine and began explaining the various choices for Charlotte's woodworking project. While they were talking, George took Helen aside.

"This will occupy Miss Richards for an hour or more. While she's busy here, I'd like to take you on a tour of the fairgrounds by gondola." When she hesitated, he added, "And I give you my word, I won't smoke."

Helen offered the beginnings of a smile. "That's very considerate of you, but I don't think I should leave Charlie here on her own. It wouldn't be right. She might think I'm tired of her company."

"She'll think no such thing. Besides, you know the very reason this building was put up was to offer a safe place for youngsters to entertain themselves while their parents or guardians are seeing the sights. I think we should take advantage of the opportunity." He paused, adding, "It won't come again."

Helen glanced at Charlie. She had already begun her

project, and was fast making friends with the other students. "Perhaps she won't mind, but I feel guilty, leaving her out. Maybe we should wait until she's finished here. She might like a gondola ride, too."

George inhaled deeply, feeling the urge to sigh in frustration, but instead he released his breath slowly and calmly. "Quite frankly, at her age, I would have found it a bore, but ask her. If she says she'd like to go with us later, we'll wait."

Charlotte was already busy at work on her piece of wood when Helen approached her. "How do you like the sloyd room, Charlie?"

She held up the block of pine that showed a freehand tracing of a lighthouse and the beginnings of her carving. "This is great fun, Mrs. Garrity!"

"You're doing a fine job. Would you like to stay here for the next hour or so?"

"If that's all right. Maybe you and Mr. Garrity could visit one of the other buildings and come back for me."

"Actually, he's suggested a gondola ride. I thought maybe we should wait for you to finish here so you could come along. What do you think?"

Charlotte looked past her teacher to George, who was waiting by the door. He gave her a big wink. She had to suppress a laugh. "To tell you the truth, Mrs. Garrity, I saw those gondolas on the lagoon when we walked to the restaurant. Don't tell Mr. Garrity, but they didn't look like much fun compared to taking the light service launch out on the big lake. I'd rather stay here, but if he wants to go on one of those silly things, you'd better go with him, or his feelings might be hurt."

"We'll be back for you later, then."

Gondola.

Within moments of stepping down to the landing in front of the Woman's Building, George had made arrangements with the gondolier, who steadied the craft while they climbed aboard.

As Helen settled beneath the velvet canopy of the long, narrow craft and the gondoliers unhurriedly propelled them over sparkling, quiet waters into North Pond, she knew George was right—she would never again witness a panorama the likes of this. She leaned back to take in the inspiring Art Building of Ionic Grecian architecture. A pillared promenade forty feet wide ran the perimeter of the classic structure. Above the gabled pediment rose a flat dome surmounted by a colossal statue of the famous figure, Winged Victory. Robert would have loved to see it. With his trained artist's eye, he had often enhanced her appreciation of the beauty around her. As she turned to look back at the Illinois Building, she realized George had been studying her.

He gave a half-smile and winked. "You have that 'missing Robert' look, Helen."

She cast a downward glance, playing with the fold of her skirt. "I'm sorry. I didn't know it was that obvious."

George patted her hand. "That's all right. You're entitled. It's only been a little over a year since he left us."

The doleful nature of his response caused Helen to look up. To her surprise, his gray eyes were watery. "You still miss him, too, don't you?"

He took his handkerchief from his pocket. Turning aside, he pretended to mop perspiration from his face, but she was certain he was drying a tear. When he faced her again, he was completely composed, giving her a hint of a smirk. "How can I miss someone who made me jealous?" he asked brusquely.

"Jealous? You? I don't believe it."

"You'd better, because it's true."

"How can that possibly be? You're a successful businessman with plenty of money, a beautiful yacht, the company of any number of friends whenever you desire. Robert often commented that you had everything you could ever want. What could he have had that could have made you jealous?"

"Robert had things money can't buy," George said regretfully.

Helen thought a moment. "He was a talented artist, and a respected member of the faculty at the university, but those things didn't seem to impress you."

George's head moved from side to side. "I never cared about being an artist."

"What, then?"

The soft rippling of the water filled the moments while George dragged up the courage for an admission he had been reluctant to make, even to himself. "He had contentment. He had you."

Helen was stunned by his words. Suddenly, none of the

things she had known about George seemed to fit anymore. Minutes lapsed while she tried to comprehend the full meaning of what he had said. Was he telling her he cared about her more than as a brother-in-law for a widowed sister-in-law?

George was the first to break the silence, regretting his outspokenness. "I shouldn't have been so blunt. Forget those things I said."

"Forget? I'm afraid it's too late for that." Troubled by her own edginess, she took a moment to compose herself. "You confuse me, George," she said calmly. "I hardly know what to believe anymore. Yesterday when we were talking on the afterdeck, you seemed strongly opposed to marriage. Now you're telling me you were jealous of your brother because of his marriage to me."

"I was full of prunes yesterday. It's taken me a long time to get up the gumption to be honest with you. At least now, you know how I really feel." They had passed the Liberal Arts Building and were entering the basin. Eager to put the subject of his feelings behind for the time being, George gestured toward a huge fountain now coming into view. "There's what I really wanted you to see this afternoon, the Columbian Fountain. That, and Mr. French's statue at the opposite end look more impressive from the water. If Robert were here, he'd be talking nonstop, explaining the meaning of all those Greek figures."

Helen smiled, willing to drop the sensitive subject of George's feelings. "I can hear him now, telling us that the one on the pedestal is Columbia, and the feminine winged figure out in front of the medieval barge is Fame. Those on each side represent the arts and sciences."

As the gondola turned past the sculpture, French's

Statue of the Republic at the opposite end of the basin came into view. Its size overwhelmed her. "It's hard to realize just how gigantic that gold-covered piece really is. I'd guess the little fingers must each be a yard long!"

"I'd like to have what they put into gold leaf for it," George said. "I read it cost fourteen hundred dollars."

"It's just like you to know the value of things. You probably know the cost of every building on the fair-grounds," Helen teased.

"Naturally. Take the Woman's Building, for instance. One hundred and thirty-eight thousand dollars were spent in construction. Then there's the Fine Arts Building—"

For the remainder of the gondola ride, Helen found her escort to be a far more delightful and entertaining conversationalist than she had ever imagined, and Robert's name didn't come up again.

When the gondola returned to the Woman's Building, George helped her to disembark, lifting her onto the landing with his hands at her waist. She felt the urge to protest, but decided not to spoil their rapport.

"I suppose our student has finished her wood project by now." George looked at his timepiece.

She checked her own watch that was hanging from her pin. "We were gone longer than I expected," she said with an edge to her voice that bespoke worry.

George took her by the elbow on the path to the Children's Building. "I'm sure she's found plenty to keep herself occupied."

Charlotte was not in the sloyd room when they looked for her there, but the moment they peeked into the gymnasium, she called to them from the balcony where she was watching as others worked out on the vaulting horses, dumbbells, bar swings, and parallel bars. "Mrs. Garrity! Up here!" She waved frantically, then ran down to meet them, her wood carving in her hand.

"Here it is! What do you think of it?"

Helen ran her fingers over the slightly squiggly outline of the light tower, the crooked beam of light that fell on the water, and the rippled lines depicting waves. "It has an interesting texture to it," she said honestly.

"Nice job, Miss Richards. I knew you could make yourself a memento here."

"This was fun. Where are we going next, Mrs. Garrity?"

Helen looked to George for an answer. "I'd best get back to my display in the Manufactures Building, so I'll leave it up to you ladies as to how to spend the last two hours of your afternoon."

"Can we come with you, Mr. Garrity?" Charlotte asked. "I'd like to see your stoves."

"Be my guests," he said, offering them each an arm.

George chose a route to the Manufactures Building which took Helen and Charlotte across a footbridge to Wooded Island, in the center of the lagoon, where shrubs, plants, and little fairy lights created an attractive, restful haven. Two more footbridges led them across Hunter's Camp, a small island, onto the mainland. To their left rose the half-mile-long façade of the building that housed George's stove display.

Charlotte thought her feet and legs would give out before they arrived at their destination, but she forgot about her fatigue when she saw the twenty-five-foot high wooden replica of an iron stove!

She dropped George's arm and rushed ahead, halting

abruptly just inside the display entrance. There stood Seth, looking neater than she had ever seen him and in a new suit of clothes, with a blond girl a little older than herself. She was standing so close as she fussed over his tie, she looked as though she were about to kiss him!

"Seth, what are you doing here? I thought you were on the *Martha G.*," Charlotte blurted out.

The blond girl turned to face her, offering a smile. "You must be Charlotte," she said sweetly.

The honey-like voice did nothing to enhance Charlotte's impression of her. Besides being friendly to a fault, she had a pretty oval face, and the lavender silk toilet she wore looked as though she had just stepped off the pages of *Harper's Bazar!*

Seth stepped forward, his hand at the girl's elbow. "Charlie, I'd like you to meet Laura Ducharme. Laura, my friend from South Manitou Island, Miss Charlotte Richards."

Laura gracefully extended her hand.

Charlotte's right arm went rigid at her side, unable to bend until a severe look from Seth prompted her to accept the handshake.

Laura's expression remained pleasant despite the minor slight. "Pleased to make your acquaintance, Miss Richards. Seth was just telling me about you. Now I must get back to Daddy's building. I hope we'll meet again before you go back to your island, Miss Richards." With a sway of her hips, she waltzed toward the door, greeted the Garritys as if they were old friends, then disappeared in the crowd.

Seth fidgeted with his celluloid collar. "How do you like my new—"

"I don't like her one bit. She had no cause to be fussing

over you like she did. As far as I could tell, your tie wasn't even crooked!"

Hands on hips, Seth stepped up to Charlotte. "Hold your tongue, young lady!"

"I'll say what I like! And I just don't happen to like your friend. The same goes for your suit!" She whirled away, nearly colliding with her teacher. With a mumbled apology, she skirted past, exiting the stove display with alacrity.

Steaming inside, Seth stalked after her, catching her by the elbow. "Maybe you don't like Laura. Maybe you don't even like my suit. The way you're acting, I doubt there's anything you *do* like. Regardless, you'd better come back to Mr. Garrity's stove display with me before you get lost and cause us all a heap of trouble looking for you."

Rigid as a mannequin, Charlotte resisted Seth's urgings.

He sighed. "I thought we were friends. I thought you listened to me. Guess I was wrong. I'll just go tell Mrs. Garrity you're tired of our company and you've run away."

He let go and walked away, praying the bluff would work. Despite an almost irresistible urge to look back, he kept his eyes on the oversized stove replica that dominated this area of the exhibition hall. At least it was visible from a long distance, in case Charlie did go off on her own.

Great snakes! Why did she have to be such an impetuous little thing, anyway? He'd never forgive himself if she really did get lost. He expected to feel her hand at his elbow at any moment.

CHAPTER 10

Confusion set in, muddling Charlotte's thoughts. She needed to sort things out quickly. She couldn't let Seth tell Mrs. Garrity she was tired of her company, but she wasn't ready to go back with him, either. Why did she dislike Laura so?

Suddenly, she realized that her feelings about Laura weren't nearly as important as her feelings about Seth. She took off after him, tugging on his sleeve as he reached the stove door.

"You're right, Seth. We *are* friends. I'm not tired of your company. I just don't care for Laura. I hope you're not mad at me. I really *do* listen to you." After a silent moment of his dead-eyed stare, she beseeched him, "Say something, Seth!"

He broke into a lopsided grin that revealed the little overlap of his front teeth. "Come on. I'm going to show you each and every one of the stoves Mr. Garrity has on display. He spent some time this morning, drilling me on them. Now I'm going to tell you everything I know."

For the next hour, Charlotte learned more than she wanted to about cooking and heating stoves. Seth carefully explained the closed stove method of bringing cold air into the appliance from beneath the floor and venting it out the top through warm air ducts, while smoke escaped through the flue. Soon enough, the afternoon came to an end, and she and Seth followed the Garritys to the exit near the Fifty-Sixth Street pier.

Charlotte was bubbling over with all she had seen her first day at the Fair. "I think I'd better ask Mrs. Garrity for some paper so I can write down a description of what I've learned while it's still fresh in my mind," she told Seth. "That way I won't forget when I tell Mama about the trip."

Though Seth was nodding his head, his attention had wandered to a carriage standing near the exit. Sitting in the back of a brougham, Charlotte quickly recognized Laura, waving her handkerchief at him. Seth waved back.

"There's my ride. I have to go now."

"I thought you were staying on the yacht!"

Seth stepped off in the direction of the waiting carriage. "Mr. Garrity has made arrangements for me to stay with Mr. Ducharme and learn about his refrigeration business. I'll see you on Monday at the Midway!"

Crestfallen, Charlotte watched him climb into the conveyance, seating himself in the back beside Laura as the driver pulled away. Maybe Seth *would* learn about refrigeration from Mr. Ducharme, but she was willing to bet he would learn a whole lot more about Laura. The thought made her so angry she wanted to shut the girl in one of her father's refrigerators and lock the door!

Over the next several days, Charlotte often wondered

how Seth was coming with his knowledge of refrigerators, and Laura, but most of the time those thoughts were overshadowed by the exciting places she visited with Mrs. Garrity at the Fair. By the evening of her fourth day at the White City, she had filled several pages with notes on her sightseeing. She sat back on her bed in the Michigan Cabin, plumped several down pillows into a mound against the knotty pine paneling, and leaned back to re-read what she had written.

July 7, 1893

The first place we visited today was the Horticulture Building. Besides the botanical displays, there was an orange grove and a lemon grove there, and a German wine cellar. My favorite part was the reproduction of the Mammoth Caves in South Dakota. It was well worth the twenty-five cents apiece Mrs. Garrity paid to gain us entrance!

Afterward, we spent quite some time looking at the foreign exhibits in the Manufactures Building. Until today, I never thought about how many different countries there are. Some of them had even set up miniature towers and buildings so you feel like you are right in that country when you visit their displays.

Switzerland was really beautiful. I would like to visit that country someday. There were three different panels painted with background scenes of lakes and mountains. One is of the Castle of Chillon. It has something to do with the poet, Byron. Another display showed beautiful watches by the hundreds!

Scene in Horticultural Building.

Germany has a really wonderful display of dolls. I know I'm supposed to be too old for them, but I would give anything for one with a porcelain face.

France has chambers that look like the salons of Louis XIV and Louis XV. There were lots of examples of perfumes, really nice furniture, stained glass, and the latest fashions from Paris.

We spent hours looking at the things made in the United States. I'll never forget the railroad train made out of eight thousand spools of silk, nor the Brooklyn Bridge constructed of fifteen hundred pounds of soap! It is thirty feet long, and it has pedestrians and vehicles crossing it, and underneath, boats on the East River.

Engine made of Silk Thread.

By the time we had seen all of this, we had only about two hours left for the Liberal Arts section. Mrs. Garrity was particularly interested in the displays by the different universities. All the important ones were represented: Harvard, Yale, Princeton, and of course, Mrs. Garrity's favorite, the University of Michigan. She introduced me to a professor who had been a good friend of her and her husband, Professor Overholt. She told him not to be surprised if he sees me as a student at the

University in five years. She has very high hopes for me!

July 8, 1893

Today we went to the Electricity Building. When we entered, we were nose to knees with a fifteen-foot high statue of Benjamin Franklin!

The General Electric Company had lots of displays in this building, but the sight I will remember most is the Edison Electric Tower. From bottom to top, it is covered with thousands of miniature lamps, and at the very top was an incandescent lamp made of hundreds of pieces of crystal.

I wish Papa could have seen the French display of arc lights used in the lighthouse service. One of them is of two hundred thousand candle power.

After the Electricity Building, we went to the Mining Building. I didn't think I'd find anything interesting there, but was I surprised. Michigan had the biggest display, and Mrs. Garrity thinks it was the most informative of any. Copper was the main feature. There were prehistoric mining tools, and a mass of native copper weighing eighty-five hundred pounds!

The last building we visited today was the Transportation Building. It has a really fancy entrance, like an arch, all carved and covered with gold leaf! Inside, the Bethlehem Iron Company put up a model of a steam hammer ninety-one feet tall! All kinds of vehicles are on display in this building. I think my favorites are the coach and sleigh of King Ludwig of Bavaria.

The Golden Doorway, Transportation Building.

July 9, 1893

We started our day in the Agriculture Building. I never realized how much grain is grown in our country. I learned an amazing fact regarding this. In 1891, our nation produced three billion, four hundred million bushels of grain!

Iowa's Corn Palace exhibit contains over one hundred types of grain. In her palace there are pyramids made of cobs, kernels, and husks.

Our next tour was of the Machinery Building. The biggest piece of machinery there is the Allis-

Corliss Engine. It produces two thousand horsepower. One of its cylinders weighs thirty tons. A man six feet tall can stand inside it without stooping!

We went next to the Art Galleries. I think Mrs. Garrity could have spent an entire day there. She surely loves art. She told me her husband might have had work represented there if he had lived. The United States, France, and Germany have the largest displays. I liked the sculptures by Calder called "Cordelia" and "Boy with Ribbon." My favorite French painting was by Degas called "Ballet Girl."

The next area of our tour was through some of the state buildings. We went to Michigan's first. On the second floor we saw examples of all the plants and flowers of the state. In another section the front pages from every newspaper and magazine had been put on display. I never knew there was so much reading material in Michigan! The most unusual item in the whole building is a piece of birch bark with a poem on it. The title was "Red Man's Rebuke," composed by the last chief of the Potawatomies.

After Michigan, we went to the largest state building at the Fair, Illinois, of course. Mrs. Garrity was particularly interested in the school exhibitions.

We managed to save just enough time for a hasty tour of the lighthouse and life-saving exhibits—

Charlotte closed her notebook and returned it to the

drawer of the writing desk. She reached for her shoes and began lacing them up, getting ready to join the Garritys on the afterdeck for the display of colored lights on the Columbian Fountain. Every night, the entertainment was more thrilling than the night before.

She wished Seth were here to see it. He was probably spending his evening with Laura. The thought rankled.

Charlotte stepped out of her cabin, made her way to the deck, and paused at the rail to watch the Ferris Wheel, all lit up and slowly turning. Tomorrow, Seth was taking *her*—not Laura—to the Midway and she would get to ride on that magnificent wheel!

CHAPTER 11

"Seth! Over here!" Charlotte spotted him from her position just inside the Midway at the eastern-most entrance off Fifty-Ninth Street, where she had been waiting with George and her teacher on this warm, sunny day. He had come a few minutes late, and the smell of popcorn and fresh roasted peanuts had already begun to whet Charlotte's appetite.

Seth was wearing the gray sack suit she had seen on him at George's stove display, and a new straw hat to shade his eyes from the bright sun. He seemed more comfortable in the celluloid collar than he had a few days earlier. His tie was perfectly knotted, which made her wonder whether Laura had helped him with it this morning.

The only thing that detracted from his appearance were the dark smudges under his eyes. Evidently, he had been working quite hard in the last few days, or perhaps he had been staying up late entertaining Laura!

"Good morning! I'm sorry I'm late," he said, adjusting his hat against the bright sun.

George laughed it off. "Wouldn't blame you if you

overslept on your day off, son. Now that you're here, I was going to suggest that you and Miss Richards go off on your own for a bit. I have some business matters to attend to at the Cold Storage Building and Helen is going with me." He fished in his pocket, pulling out a fistful of coins. When he opened his palm, Charlotte tried to count them, but there were too many. He picked out a five-dollar gold piece, which he handed to Seth. "There you go, son. The spending money I promised. You've earned it."

"Thank you, sir."

George separated several half dollars from his remaining loose change and offered them to Charlotte. "Here's a little change for some trinkets."

She wanted to accept, but her conscience overruled. She had saved half of the five dollars her mother had given her for today. "Thank you, Mr. Garrity, but I already have spending money."

"What was it you wanted to do most, Miss Richards? Ride the Ferris Wheel?"

She nodded.

"No Ferris Wheel until you take these coins off my hands."

"But . . . "

"I mean it!"

Charlotte didn't think he would carry out his threat, but neither did she want to argue further. "I'm only taking them because you insist. Thank you, Mr. Garrity."

"Seth, I'm holding you responsible for Miss Richards's well-being."

"I'll see to it she doesn't get lost, or in any trouble, sir," he promised, certain that despite Charlie's penchant for mischief, the task would be a cinch after the tough jobs he'd encountered since leaving South Manitou Island.

George consulted his pocket watch. "Seth, I'd like you to see some of the equipment at the Cold Storage Building. Why don't you and Miss Richards meet us there at twelve." He pulled a map out of his pocket and pointed to its location. "It's right here, next to the Sixty-Fourth Street entrance. You can take the elevated railroad and get off at the Transportation Building."

Seth studied the map. "We'll be there, sir."

"Enjoy the Ferris Wheel, Charlie," said Mrs. Garrity.

She was already pulling on Seth's arm in the direction of that attraction. The crowd was beginning to thicken, the air abuzz with foreign languages and accents—an Irish brogue as they passed the Irish Village, Oriental voices from the Japanese bazaar, against the rhythm of strange drums from far-off lands. Across the way, the restaurants fronting Hagenbeck's Trained Animal Building sent up the aroma of fried foods. Seth seemed to be dragging his heels. "What's the matter? Didn't you get any sleep last night?" she wanted to know. "You've got circles under your eyes the likes of which I've never seen before."

"I slept last night, but not long enough, I guess."

"I thought you'd be rested today, since yesterday was Sunday. Or did you have to work then, too? What have you been doing since I last saw you, anyway?"

"Charlie, you ask too many questions," he said crossly.

"No need to get angry. It's just that I've been wondering what you've been up to for the last four days."

"I've been working for Mr. Ducharme and some of the men involved with Mr. Garrity's stove sales here in Chicago."

"But what did you *do?*"

"I helped to deliver some stoves, and I put in some time in Mr. Ducharme's foundry to see how sand castings are made." From the puzzled look on her face, he could tell she didn't fully understand his answer. Before she could ask more, he quickened his pace, determined to take the lead, both physically and conversationally. "Come on now, don't dawdle. Let's get to the Ferris Wheel before the crowd."

Within minutes, Charlotte found herself in a short line for the ride. The conductor put her and Seth into one of the glassed-in cars, then locked their door.

"This car could hold at least . . . "

"Sixty people," Seth finished for her.

"But we have it all to ourselves. Aren't we lucky!" Too excited to sit, she paced the length of the car from one end to the other as it began to rise. When the Ferris Wheel paused to take on more passengers, she took out her map to identify the buildings in the Midway and on the grounds proper. She could look across at the twin towers of the Chinese Theater to the west. Opposite that, a reproduction of the City of Vienna had sprung up, its *rathhause*, or city hall standing proud with its clock tower. Nearly three dozen other buildings stood shoulder to shoulder with it, forming a quaint square with an open-air café.

She paced again to the opposite end of the car, looking past the reproduction of the Eiffel Tower to two obelisks. There, another foreign settlement captured her attention. "Look at that, Seth! Those people are getting on a camel. We *must* go there and take a ride!"

Seth chuckled at the awkwardness of the couple when the animal began to rise. "I'll take you to Cairo Street, but you have to promise to go up in the captive balloon with me." He pointed in the direction of the Chinese Towers where the inflated aircraft was rising. "The Ferris Wheel goes to a height of two hundred and sixty-four feet. The balloon goes up fourteen hundred ninety-two feet, in honor of the year Columbus discovered America."

"Boy, you're smart! How did you learn all that?"

"Laura told me," Seth promptly admitted. "She says the view from the balloon is spectacular!"

"Oh, hush!" Charlotte snapped. She went back to watching out the window. The tethered balloon was ascending high above them. Obviously, Laura was right. The view from there would be fantastic. "Do you suppose we'll be able to see South Manitou Island from the balloon?"

Seth laughed. "Not quite. The earth is curved, so the horizon will be a lot closer than that. It should be a spectacular view of the lake on a clear day like today, though."

Not far from the Ferris Wheel, a circular building with the statue of a goddess in front drew Charlotte's attention. On the building was inscribed, "Hawaii Kil'auea." She couldn't make out the words beneath it.

"What do you suppose goes on there?"

"If you go inside, you feel like you're in a volcano. There's smoke, and flames, and rumblings. You wouldn't like it."

"How do you know? Did Laura tell you that?"

He simply grinned.

"Laura doesn't know what I'd like. I think we should see the volcano."

Charlotte continued to study the view, discovering a German Village to the east of Cairo Street. "Look at the castle!" she marveled. "It even has a mote and drawbridges!" She stared in fascination, eager to gain entrance once they returned to solid ground.

"There's the Irish castle, farther down," Seth pointed out.

Charlotte could pick out two gray towers of a medieval gateway opening on a village that had a round tower in its center. "There's so much to see, we'll never get to it all," she groaned. Their car had reached the top of the wheel, and she began studying the view of the grounds proper. "I wish you could have been with Mrs. Garrity and me when we visited the other exhibits. You would have loved the 'Lord of the Isles' in the Transportation Building."

"That's the wide-gauge engine that set the world's speed record on the daily run between London and Bath, isn't it?"

Charlotte's jaw dropped, but she quickly overcame her surprise. "Isn't there anything Laura didn't tell you about the Fair?"

He raised his brow. "I'm not at liberty to say."

"Not at liberty to say? What kind of talk is that?" she asked, then grudgingly conceded, "at least Laura's smart, as well as being pretty."

While the wheel continued its rotation, nonstop this time now that all its passengers were loaded, Charlotte pointed out the various buildings and briefly told what she had seen in them, from the huge dome of the Horticulture Building to the vast expanse of the Manufactures and Liberal Arts Building, to the Electricity and Mining Buildings, the single-story Agriculture Building, and—dainty compared to the rest—the towered Michigan Building.

Reluctantly, she left their car when the conductor opened its door. Unlike her descent from the heights of the light tower on South Manitou, it felt strange to set her feet on the ground again. She stood still for a moment, collecting her bearings.

Seth steadied Charlotte by the elbow, turning her toward the balloon park. "That's the direction we want to head next. Let's see if we can get tickets for the next ascension."

The Chinese Village, with its bazaar of rich silks and embroideries, elaborately decorated table and toilet wares, ivory whatnots, and expensive teas, was just too enticing to pass up. "Seth, you've just got to let me look for a few minutes."

He scowled.

"The balloon won't be down for a while," she argued, pointing to the craft still several hundred feet aloft.

"All right, but only for a few minutes."

In the short time allotted her, Charlotte purchased small silk embroideries for her mother, Aurora, and Bridget for a modest amount. The tiny, intricate stitches depicting pagodas, flowers, and birds were a fascinating study in artistic needlework.

At the entrance to the balloon park, Seth hesitated in front of a sign, reading it aloud: "Admission—twenty-five cents. Balloon ascensions—"

"Two dollars!" Charlotte blurted out. "Maybe your friend, Laura, is rich enough to pay that price, but I have no intention of taking a balloon ride that costs two dollars. The Ferris Wheel was good enough for me."

Seth silently admitted to himself that Charlotte was right, and turned away. "What shall we do then? There's time for one or two adventures before we meet the Garritys."

Captive Balloon Park.

"I suppose, if we're not going up in the balloon, we won't ride on the camel, either," she lamented.

"I knew there was a good side to this predicament," he bantered. "Laura said the camel ride was only for fools, anyway."

"I should have known she wouldn't like it. Miss *Harper's Bazar* was probably afraid she'd muss her dress!"

Seth didn't argue.

As they worked their way back toward the Ferris Wheel, the polygonal-shaped building Charlotte had seen from above reminded her of their earlier discussion. "This is the perfect time to take the trip to Hawaii, down into the crater of a volcano." She gazed at the large statue she had seen from the Ferris Wheel. It looked even more gigantic from ground level. "Pele, goddess of fire," she read on the side of the building. "Greatest volcano on earth in action. Nine miles around, one thousand feet deep . . . burning lakes." She grabbed Seth by the sleeve. "Come on. Let's go inside!"

In contrast to the description, pleasant music issued forth from the canopy in front of the building, where a choir—Kanak musicians, according to the sign—drew an appreciative audience.

Within minutes, Charlotte and Seth were in the round theater. The lights dimmed. From complete darkness, the volcanic recreation began to play against the curved walls, illuminating two huge, snowcapped peaks, and opposite those, the Pacific Ocean, its waves lit by a full moon, their undulating surfaces glittering like silver.

The Goddess of Fire, Pele.

The next vision to surround them was the precipitous, irregular wall inside the fiery mountain. Above were bubbling, seething pools, lakes of fire, tall jagged crags, toppling masses of rocks, and outpourings of lava flowing along in hissing, smoking streams! It was so real, Charlotte reached out to Seth, grabbing hold of his arm. Below her yawned a fathomless pit, belching huge puffs of smoke. Everywhere, cracks and fissures opened, threatening to swallow her up! She tightened her grip on Seth.

From the ragged edges of the crater licked fierce flames emitting sulfurous gases. With them came froth and spume, and glassy threads. Someone behind Charlotte said they were Pele's hair.

An inky lake of molten lava pulsed and throbbed, suddenly bursting forth in a sea of fire! The center of the flames were white, yellow, golden in their fury, tinged with crimson and green, then fading at the edges to dull red. Above it hung a curtain of smoke, and in the distance, a dull rumbling punctuated by deafening explosions that played bass to a descant of hissings and growlings. When the floor beneath Charlotte seemed to move with the force of the eruption, she leaned on Seth to maintain her balance.

Gradually, the volcanic activity died down and the crater went to sleep.

Charlotte let go of Seth and stepped outside. Systematically she began checking her skirt, from waistband to hem, carefully examining each panel. Then she inspected the sleeves and front of her shirtwaist.

"That fire was so real, I was sure I got scorched," she told Seth.

He rolled his eyes. "Enough of your foolishness. It's time to meet the Garritys."

At first glimpse, Charlotte considered the Cold Storage Building to be rather uninteresting in design. Tucked along the west border of the fairgrounds near the railroad tracks, its nearly windowless, boxy architecture excited little attention, and would have looked like any other warehouse except for the towers at each corner, and the fifth, large central tower that rose five stories, offering an observation platform.

As Charlotte approached the site with Seth, she realized that the main entrance, a massive Roman arch supported by eight columns, was the only ornamented feature on the structure. Beneath its graceful, curve the Garritys were

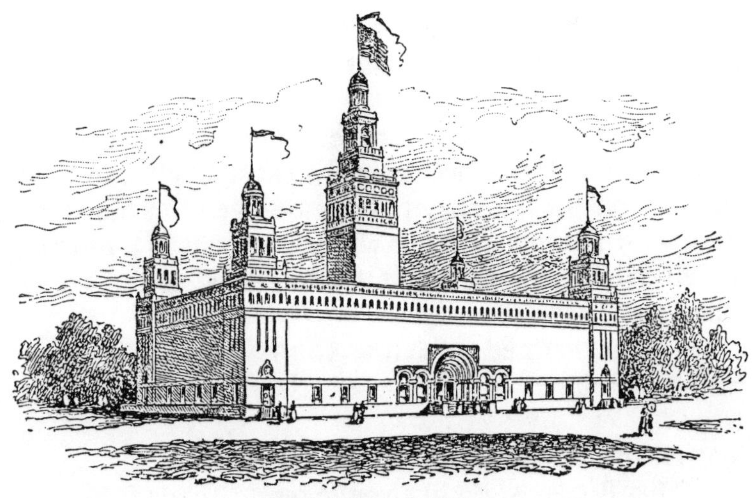
The Cold Storage Building.

waiting, as George had promised, and along with them, two others—a gentleman of approximately George's age, and Laura Ducharme!

Seething, Charlotte stopped dead. "Why didn't you tell me we were meeting Laura?"

"I had no idea she would be here. Honest!"

"I refuse to go near her!"

"Her father and Mr. Garrity do a lot of business together. *Please* don't cause any trouble."

"I said I won't have anything to do with her!"

Seth placed his hands firmly on her shoulders, fixing her with the foreboding stare of hazel eyes that had turned muddy with anger. "Charlotte Richards, you are going to be polite to Laura or I will take you over my knee right in front of her!"

So infuriated was Seth that his thumbs dug painfully into Charlotte's shoulders. She drew a tight breath. "All right. I'll do as you say. But I won't like it. Not for a minute."

Unwillingly, she approached Laura with Seth at her side, trying not to notice the girl's exceedingly expensive and fashionable blazer suit of white serge. Her blond hair was caught up beneath her white straw hat in a fetching style. When she offered Seth a dazzling smile, it made Charlotte's stomach turn.

George seemed oblivious to the tension Charlotte brought with her. "You found us without any trouble, I trust?"

"No trouble, Mr. Garrity," she answered meekly.

"Miss Richards, I'd like you to meet Laura's father, Mr. Ducharme," George said.

"Pleased to make your acquaintance." Charlotte offered her hand to Mr. Ducharme, a dark-haired, clean-shaven man whose tall, handsome form did justice to his perfectly tailored blue pinstripe suit.

He bent slightly at the waist when he took her hand. "Welcome to my Cold Storage Building."

"Did you enjoy the Midway?" The words flowed so sweetly from Laura's tongue, Charlotte expected a swarm of bees to surround the girl at any moment. Worse yet, Laura's smile could have melted the polar ice cap.

Charlotte tried to respond, but her jaw locked up tight.

"We just came from the Hawaiian volcano," Seth answered. "Charlotte was enthralled by the experience. I could tell by the way she clutched my arm."

Laura's genuinely mirthful laugh had Seth laughing with her. Charlotte wanted to scream, but she had promised Seth she would behave, so she pasted on a smile to hide her clenched teeth.

"Let's go inside," George suggested. "I'd like to show Seth a few things before our one o'clock reservation for lunch at the Café de Marine."

Seth fell into step with Laura, and Helen and George followed, leaving Charlotte to walk alone. Well, no matter. Beside Laura, Charlotte's practical walking suit looked downright dowdy.

From the front portal, they passed into a huge engine room so noisy that Charlotte could barely hear Mr. Ducharme describing the massive Hercules machines to Seth. Laura took her father aside and shouted a question only he could understand. He nodded in reply, then she turned to Charlotte and motioned for her to follow.

Charlotte hesitated, but decided even Laura's company would be more pleasant than the painful racket.

When they had left the roar behind, Laura explained, "I want to take you to the fifth floor where Daddy's skating rink and restaurant are under construction. It's quite interesting, and not nearly so noisy. To tell you the truth, those Hercules machines always give me a headache."

Charlotte couldn't fault Laura there. Her own head was beginning to throb.

She followed Laura to an elevator in the central tower. When the door closed, it sped to the top.

They stepped out onto the fifth floor hallway, which was cluttered with workmen's tools. Charlotte immediately noticed an unusual odor. "Miss Ducharme—"

"Please call me Laura. Is it all right if I call you Charlotte? After all Seth has told me, I feel like I know you."

The revelation came as no surprise. "That would be fine . . . Laura. I was about to ask if you smelled—"

Before Charlotte could complete her question, a man shouted from another hallway.

"Fire! Everybody out!"

CHAPTER 12

"This way, Charlotte!" Laura headed down a hallway next to the elevator.

Charlotte followed, picking her way past hammers, saws, wrenches and tool boxes. A thin veil of smoke drifted above her. She waved it away with one hand and lifted her skirt with the other, doing her best to keep up with Laura.

The smoke thickened, making her eyes burn, and breathing nearly impossible. Charlotte held her breath and tried to see through the poisonous haze. Her hand against the wall, she felt her way to the end of the hallway, only to discover it ran dead end into another. Looking first to the left, then to the right, she could make out neither the young woman nor the workmen through the gray cloud.

"Laura?" Her voice sounded pitifully weak, even to her own ears. A fit of coughing overcame her, but she was determined to make herself heard. She knelt down on the floor where the air was clearer and forced a deep breath into her lungs. "Laura . . . where are you?" she gasped.

She crawled along the hallway to the right, coming to a

closed door. It was warm to her touch. She could hear the crackling of flames. Urgently, she crept on, scrambling over hammers, nails, screwdrivers, and scraps of lumber.

She reached an opening on her right. It was filled with smoke. Clouds of it seemed to rush at her. She felt along the floor ahead of her and discovered a step.

The stairway! But how could she make it down five flights of stairs in this thick haze? She had no choice. This stairway was her only means of escape. Feeling for the railing, she looped one leg over the top, turned on her stomach, and prayed for a soft landing.

"These three Hercules machines weigh a hundred and twenty tons apiece," Mr. Ducharme shouted above the roar, obviously proud of his equipment. "Over there is one of the dynamos for arc and incandescent lighting. There's another on the opposite end."

Seth took his time looking over the mammoth engines. He'd never seen the likes of them. He wished his father were here to appreciate them. It was just as well Laura had offered to show Charlie some of the more interesting features of the yet-to-be-completed building. She would have no interest at all in this kind of tour.

"Come with me and I'll show you how ice is being made," said Mr. Ducharme, heading off to the left of the giant machines. The noise lessened as they followed him to a different compartment.

"I'm thinking of investing in the refrigeration business," George told Seth when talking became easier.

"He and Mr. Ducharme have been discussing the possibilities all morning long," said Helen. "I think George was trying to convince himself, more than me, that it's a good idea."

"You mean you're against—" George's question was interrupted by Laura's panicked cry.

"Papa! Everybody! The building's on fire!"

"Where's Charlie?" asked Seth.

Laura's blue eyes were full of fear. "I don't know! We had just stepped off the elevator onto the fifth floor when someone said a fire had started. I told Charlotte to follow me. I headed toward the stairs. When I got down to the fourth floor, I realized I had lost her. I tried to go back, but . . . " her voice cracked. "The smoke . . . it was so thick . . . I couldn't find her!" Laura began to cry.

Mr. Ducharme put his arm about his daughter's shoulders, turning her toward the exit at the front of the building. "Take it easy, sweetheart. You did your best. There's nothing more we can do but get out of here and call the firemen."

Seth's heart filled with fear. He stepped off in the opposite direction. "I'm going after Charlie!"

"No, Seth!" George protested.

"I've got to." He started at a run.

"Ducharme, see that Helen gets out of here," George ordered. He took off after Seth. The fleet-footed boy was already several yards ahead of him. George tried to run, but his huge gut slowed him down. He pressed against it with one hand, swinging the other arm to increase his momentum. His stumpy legs could manage strides only half the length of Seth's. He sucked his breath in short gasps. At least he had one huge advantage over the boy. He knew the building.

By now, Seth had reached the iron gate of the elevator which rested on the first floor. *Lord, no! Please don't let him get in!* George prayed.

Seth looked first to his right, then to his left, evidently debating which way to turn.

"Seth!—" George gasped for air. "This way to the stairs!" he lied, hoping the boy would take the bait. His heart raced, his face grew hot, his lungs burned, but new energy burst forth when Seth headed toward him. "Through here!" He indicated a door.

The moment the boy came close enough, George collared him with a strong arm. "Sorry, son . . . I can't let you go up there." He wrestled the wiry boy through a door that exited to the outside.

"Let me go!"

Ducharme came to George's rescue, forcing Seth's arms behind his back. "Don't try to be a hero, Seth. Leave that to the ones who are trained for it. The firemen are on their way."

With Ducharme's help, George muscled Seth away from the door.

The lad stopped struggling and gazed up at the building. "The tower's on fire!"

George glanced up, relaxing his grip. Smoke was seeping from the top level.

With one violent twist, Seth broke and ran toward the door.

"Seth! No!" George shouted, starting after him again.

Ducharme caught his friend by the arm. "Don't go, George. There's nothing more you can do."

He watched helplessly as Seth disappeared inside the building.

Once inside, Seth ran from door to door until he found the one to the stairway. A small bulb lit the stairwell.

There was no sign of smoke on the first floor, and only a thin haze just above that. He took the steps two at a time up to the second floor, then to the third.

The smoke thickened. He could barely see. He took his handkerchief from his pocket and held it over his nose, drew a thin breath of the foul air, closed his eyes against the irritating haze, and began to climb another flight. When he reached the landing, his foot encountered something soft. He half-opened his eyes. There lay Charlie, limp as a rag doll!

He scooped her up and took the stairs as quickly as he could. He was below the second floor when the electricity went off, leaving him in pitch darkness. He slowed his pace. He couldn't afford any false steps. And he couldn't waste time. The smoke was thickening, closing off his lungs!

Helen's nerves were so taut, she pressed her hands over her mouth to suppress a scream. She could only think that Charlie had been entrusted to her care, and she had betrayed that trust. How would she ever explain the girl's death to her mother? And what of Seth? He wouldn't have come on the trip, except that she had recommended him to George. She started toward the door.

George quickly caught up with her, taking her by the elbow, pulling her around to face him. "Have you lost your mind, woman? You can't go in there!"

She tried to twist free, but George's grip tightened severely, bruising her. She thrashed at him. "Let go! You're hurting me!"

"I won't let you die in there! Now stop fighting me, or you'll hurt yourself even more!"

Temporarily, Helen ceased her struggle. A few feet away, Laura clung to her father. In the distance, fire bells clanged. Within moments, equipment rolled into place. Firemen jumped down from their rigs and began unrolling hoses.

Helen tried again to free herself from George's iron grip. "I've got to tell them about Charlie! Maybe they can find her!"

"Let Laura do that. She knows better what to tell them than you do," George reasoned. He forced Helen farther away from the building.

The Ducharmes spoke with the fire chief, then joined Helen and George to watch and wait. A crowd started to gather.

Several firefighters worked in concert, manning hoses. Another two dozen men ran inside the building, and in less than two minutes, reappeared on the tower balcony.

Helen watched intently. Suddenly, flames broke out below the balcony.

"Oh, no," Ducharme groaned.

George's grip on Helen went slack as his attention focused on the flames.

Where's Charlie? The question haunted Helen. Every fiber of her being told her to run back inside.

Don't do it! the voice of reason told her. *You'll surely perish!*

No sooner had that thought passed from her mind, than a tremendous explosion rent the air! Before her eyes, the tower collapsed, taking at least two score of firemen with it into a gaseous flame! She screamed. Laura cried out.

Yards away, two firemen blasted the center of the upper story with water. Their attempt seemed pitiful.

Helen hid her head on George's shoulder. How could she possibly face losing Charlie?

"Mrs. Garrity! Over there!" Laura's voice cut through the fog in Helen's mind. She lifted her head. Laura was pointing to a litter being set on the ground by Seth and a fireman.

She ran to them. Charlie's face was puffy and smudged. She was only semi-conscious, moaning something about a volcano, but she was alive!

Helen knelt opposite Seth and reached for Charlie's hand.

Seth grabbed her by the wrist. "Careful, Mrs. Garrity. Charlie's right hand is badly burned."

She looked up into Seth's hazel eyes. "Thank the good Lord you found her!"

"Some would call me a fool," he said wryly.

Helen shook her head. Again, she focused on her student. Charlie's breathing was noisy, labored, as if she were struggling for air. Her right hand was beginning to swell with blisters. Helen took Charlie's left hand in hers for a moment and pressed it to her lips.

Charlie's eyes opened through swollen slits. She mumbled something unintelligible, then drifted into semi-consciousness again.

Behind her, George, Laura, and Ducharme carried on a discussion. Helen rose and listened.

"I'll call the doctor and tell him to bring his nurse and meet us at my place," Ducharme suggested. "Miss Richards will get better care at home than in a hospital."

"Charlotte can stay in my bedroom, Mr. Garrity," Laura offered.

"No need," George countered. "Ducharme, if you'll loan your carriage, we can take her to my Aunt Mercy's. She and Mother can help with the nursing."

"I'll help, too," Helen offered.

George nodded and turned to Ducharme again. "Could you tell your doctor to meet us at the Spencers' place on Lakeshore Drive?"

"Consider it done. And while I'm at it, I'd better cancel our luncheon reservation at the Café de Marine."

Seth walked the length of the drawing room of Mercy Spencer's Lakeshore Drive mansion, turned around at the bookcase and retraced his steps, keeping one eye and both ears on the front stairs. Certainly, the doctor would finish with Charlie soon and come down to give his prognosis. Ducharme and Laura were in the front parlor. Seth had been there with them until they banished him for his incessant pacing.

From the window, he could see George circling the courtyard, stooping now and then to pluck a wilted petal from what appeared to be a perfectly tended garden. He had been an absolute bear where Charlie was concerned, carrying her to the carriage, insisting on riding with her, putting everyone else but Helen in a hack. George had even threatened the doctor when he showed up at the front door, warning what he'd do to him if he didn't treat Charlie right.

Helen, Martha, and Mercy were upstairs helping the doctor and his nurse with Charlie. At least she was in good hands, but she had not been fully conscious when they had put her into the carriage at the Cold Storage Building, or what was left of it. Seth was fairly certain she had bumped her head before he had found her on the landing. When would she wake up and be able to talk to him? He wanted to know she was going to be all right.

What seemed like an eternity had actually amounted to only an hour when Dr. Zimmer descended the curving stairs. George had come in to wait with Seth, and cut him off on the way to the stairs, squeezing his bulky shoulders through the drawing room door in an effort to reach the doctor first.

Everyone converged on the front hall before the doctor had even reached the first floor. The instant he appeared, they all spoke at once.

"How is she?"

"Will she be all right?"

"Is she in much pain?"

"Is she conscious?"

"Be patient, *bitte*," the short, stocky doctor pleaded as he descended, stopping on the next to the last step. "She is sometimes awake, sometimes not. She has a bump on *der kopf*." He put his hand to his forehead. "It vill go down, in time, but she should suffer no lasting effects. She has much pain from her burns. I give her medicine. She is now asleep. I come back tomorrow to change bandages. Until then, Frau Mercy, Frau Martha, and Frau Helen vill care for her."

Seth shoved past George. "Can I go up and see her?"

"Vat is your name, *bitte*?"

"Seth."

"Ah! Seth! When Fraulein Charlie vas avake, she ask for Seth. Yah, you can see her."

Seth started up the stairs, but the doctor stopped him

with a hand against his chest. "Tomorrow."

Seth slept very little, owing to the cot Mercy had assigned to him on the second floor of the carriage house and his worry over Charlie. When morning came, he encountered Martha in the front hallway as he was about to climb the stairs.

"You're not to go up there until Dr. Zimmer has paid his call," she stated adamantly. "I stayed by Miss Richards' side most of the night. Helen has taken over her care. I'm going up to get some rest. You're welcome to wait in the drawing room."

"Yes, ma'am."

Seth waited a while, then snuck up the back stairs. Stealthily, he made his way through the hallway to the bedroom. When Helen saw him outside the door, she left Charlie's side to speak with him.

"The doctor gave her something for the pain yesterday, but I think it's wearing off. Sometimes, she blinks her eyes open, then falls asleep again. Go on in and see her. I'll be in the room across the hall if you need me."

Seth entered the room and bent over the bed in which Charlie lay. It was a huge, imposing affair with posts that reached nearly to the ceiling, its canopy frame dripping with white silk fringe that edged the satin-striped, gauze-like fabric. The high, plump mattress, fluffy pillows, and generous satin bedclothes nearly swallowed her slender form. He took her limp hand in his and stroked her fingers, listening to her every shallow, labored breath.

So many things he wanted to tell her. So many things she was still too young to understand.

She was a bother. She was an angel. She was a sister.

She was a friend. She was a tomboy. She was a beauty. She made him laugh. She made him cry. She made him angry. She made him glad. She made life difficult. She made life fun. She made him loathe her. She made him love her.

So many words he wanted to say. So many feelings he dared not share.

"Charlie?" he whispered softly. "Charlie, it's me, Seth."

He waited, hope against hope, for her to show some sign of recognition. If only she would wake up and say his name! But minutes later, not even an eyelash had flickered.

"Charlie, you probably won't believe this," he continued in a whisper, "but I wish I could trade places with you. I can't stand seeing you this way. You've got to get over this, Charlie." He leaned down and touched his lips to her cheek. It wasn't even a kiss. Not really.

Her eyelids twitched.

His heart hammered.

"Charlie? Are you awake? Say something, Charlie. *Please!*"

CHAPTER 13

Charlotte struggled to raise her lids. She felt as though she couldn't move. Her entire body possessed half the strength of an exhausted flea. She tried again to open her eyes and managed to blink. In that brief glimpse, she realized someone was standing over her. Seth? It looked like him, with his hair waving over his forehead.

She worked to open her eyes partway. She felt dizzy, as if she were suspended, floating on a cloud of white silk high above the floor. There was a cloud above her, too. Was this heaven? No, it couldn't be. There was a painting on the wall behind Seth. A very crooked painting. Or maybe it was straight, and she was seeing things cockeyed.

Whose room was this, anyway? She couldn't seem to make sense of anything, nor could she keep her eyes open any longer. Though she could hear her name, she couldn't get her tongue to work.

She felt a pressure on her left hand. A squeeze. Several squeezes. They kept coming in a pattern, over and over. Three long ones together, then another set of three in a long-short-long pattern. Squeeze . . . squeeze . . . squeeze. Squeeze . . . half-squeeze . . . squeeze.

A light flickered before her closed eyes—lantern light from a storm-tossed boat coming toward the lighthouse. It came in a rhythm—three longs, then long-short-long. *O.K.* It was Mr. Trevelyn's signal that he was coming home safely, a pattern Seth had taught her when she had first come to live at the keeper's quarters on South Manitou Island.

Charlotte concentrated all her energy in the hand Seth was holding. He repeated the pattern of squeezes.

"Charlie? Can you hear me? Please say something, Charlie!"

Very slowly, very weakly, she squeezed his hand three times. After a pause, she managed three more squeezes in a long-short-long pattern.

Seth's heart raced. Until now, he had not really been certain she was all right. With a soaring spirit, he whispered, "Thanks be!"

"Seth?"

Though Charlie's voice was barely audible, he knew of no sweeter sound. "Charlie, are you all right? Can I get you something? How do you feel?" he asked urgently, regretting the manner in which he had bombarded her with questions.

Her eyes blinked open, and seemed to focus on him. Her mouth turned upward, a hint of her mischievous grin lurking at the corners. "Seth . . . where am I? Where's Laura?"

"You're at Mr. Garrity's aunt's house. Laura is home."

Charlotte's expression became peaceful momentarily, then, below the bump that had popped out on the left side of her forehead, she frowned. "Seth, are you mad at me for . . . you know . . . causing all this trouble? I tried to follow Laura. I couldn't see . . . the smoke . . . I tried to slide down the stairs . . . I don't remember how I got—"

"Oh, Charlie!" he moaned. "It wasn't your fault. I'm just glad you're safe now."

After a quiet moment, she asked, "Seth, how . . . did I get . . . out of the fire?"

"Someone carried you out."

"You?" she asked, and when he didn't answer, she concluded, "It was you, wasn't it?"

Seth kept silent.

"You're awfully good to me. Better than a brother," she half-whispered.

He was glad her eyes had drifted shut so she wouldn't see the tears welling in his own. He tried to speak past the lump in his throat, but it was impossible. His words were trapped inside. *I love you, Charlie. I didn't even know it until today.* He gently squeezed her hand once again.

Her mouth drew into a half-smile that lingered. He stayed there, holding her hand. When Helen came in to take up her vigil once again, Charlotte was slumbering peacefully.

The next time Charlotte's eyes opened, Seth was gone. Martha Garrity was there instead, straightening the picture on the wall that had appeared crooked the last time she looked. When the woman turned toward her, Charlotte closed her eyes, feigning sleep. She may have been through a fire since the last time she had seen George Garrity's mother, but even that had not erased the memory of her last encounter with the feisty lady.

Martha's silk skirt rustled softly, and Charlotte could tell without looking that she had settled into the chair beside her bed. How Charlotte wished the woman would go away and send in her daughter-in-law. Her stomach was beginning to growl.

She could see a poached egg sitting pretty on a piece of toast. Her mouth nearly watered at the vision, but she would not ask Martha Garrity for it. That woman probably had other ideas about what a patient needed for her first meal during recovery.

"I know you're awake, Miss Richards," Martha said quietly. "Are you hungry? The doctor is coming soon to check on you. I'd like to be able to tell him you've taken nourishment."

When Charlotte didn't answer, Martha continued.

"Cook will make you anything you'd like. The sooner you eat, the sooner you will recover," she reasoned, her tone completely absent of cynicism. "Perhaps you would care for some cambric tea, or porridge, or—"

Charlotte's eyes opened. "Poached egg on toast?"

Martha's brows shot up, then she quickly covered her surprise. "Of course. Would you like something to drink with it?"

"Milk would be fine, thank you."

Martha started to leave, then turned back, fussing with the satin bedclothes, tucking in here, smoothing out wrinkles there. "Are you comfortable? Can I fluff your pillows?"

Charlotte leaned forward. "I suppose they could use some fluffing," she said, beginning to enjoy the attention.

One at a time, Martha shook air into the three pillows and replaced them behind Charlotte's back with a pat.

"There. Now I'll see to your poached egg on toast. In the meantime, I'll send my daughter-in-law in. She'll be glad to know you're awake."

When the woman had reached the bedroom door, Charlotte said, "Mrs. Garrity? There's one thing more."

Martha pirouetted. "Yes, Miss Richards?"

"Mrs. Garrity, I just wanted to say—"

"Just name it. I'll see to it you have it."

Charlotte swallowed, then started over. "I just wanted to say that if you were like this all the time, I think I could really get to like you."

"Thank you . . . I think."

Helen sat with Charlotte while she ate her poached egg on toast. As the teacher retold the events of the last twenty-four hours, she realized they had seemed more like a hundred and twenty-four. Helen had slept barely two hours since the fire, so anxious was she about her star pupil. Though she still felt somewhat jittery, the return of Charlie's appetite meant the worst of the crisis had passed. Perhaps now, with the recovery well underway, they could both get back to feeling somewhat normal.

Charlotte was glad Martha had sent her daughter-in-law up with the tray of food, despite the new truce she seemed to have struck with the older woman. It was a struggle to eat with her left hand, and if she were going to be messy, she preferred being so in the company of her teacher.

Despite having to learn to use a fork all over again, she managed to wipe her plate clean in due time. And the cold, refreshing milk helped to ease the discomfort of her dry, parched throat. When she had finished, her teacher took her tray from her lap, set it outside the door on a table in the hallway, then returned to continue their conversation.

"I'll send your mother a telegram as soon as the doctor has come to see you. I hesitated to send one yesterday, for fear of alarming her unnecessarily. Is there anything you would like to tell her?"

Charlotte thought for a minute. How she wished she were home, on her island! Her mother knew just how to nurse her when she was sick, and there was no place like her own bed beside the window that looked out on the light tower, and the comforting scent of rosewater when her dolly lay next to her.

This spacious room in the Spencer home was too grand to be cozy, with its oversize Empire bed. Its plaster walls were painted cool white, the hardwood floor was bare except for two small white scatter rugs, and the smell of carbolic acid served as a constant reminder that this was a sick room.

Not that Martha and her teacher hadn't done everything they could for her—they had certainly been very kind—but the Spencers' city home just wasn't like the keeper's quarters. Nevertheless, she couldn't put all that in a telegram.

Then she remembered the words her mother had spoken the night before she had departed from the island. She hadn't understood them until now, but they would get her message across perfectly. "Here's what I'd like to tell Mama—that I miss her, that she shouldn't worry, and that soon I'll come back to her safe and sound, just the way I was when I left." She raised her bandaged right hand and studied it a moment, adding, "Well, almost the same. When will I be able to go home, Mrs. Garrity?"

Helen recognized a hint of longing in Charlie's voice. "Dr. Zimmer would like you to stay here until the bandage comes off. That will be in about a week. He said you could go sooner, except that we have no doctors on the island. I'm sorry you're stuck here for the time being, Charlie. Maybe I shouldn't have invited you to the Fair."

The note of despair in her teacher's voice, as well as the words, lit a spark inside Charlotte. She sat straight up and looked directly into her eyes, red with fatigue and slightly watery. "Oh, yes! You should have! I'm glad you did!"

It was all Helen could do to keep her tears from spilling over.

The evening before the *Martha G.* was to depart for the return trip to South Manitou Island, Seth came to see Charlotte. She had hoped he would be alone this time, but just as on his previous visits, Laura was with him. And as before, the Ducharmes' driver brought them in one of her father's fancy rigs, this time a cabriolet.

With Seth and Laura gathered around the white wicker table in the lamplit courtyard, Charlotte tried to tell herself it didn't really matter that Laura's *Harper's Bazar* wardrobe still made her self-conscious. After tonight, she would likely never see the girl again. Best of all, neither would Seth.

Cook brought a tray of pink lemonade and fancy English biscuits, then left the three of them alone.

Seth turned to Laura, a strange look passing between them. Charlotte sensed an undercurrent and broke the silence, working hard to keep from sounding smug. "Laura, I suppose you'll miss Seth a great deal once he's gone, won't you?"

Laura's smile reminded Charlotte of the copy of the Mona Lisa she had once studied in a book her teacher had loaned her. She sipped her lemonade, saying nothing.

Seth gulped down his beverage, then asked, "Laura, would you please go in and ask Cook if she has another pitcher of this delicious pink lemonade? I have quite a thirst tonight."

Without a word, Laura acquiesced. Seth's eyes followed her graceful movements until she reached the door, a reminder to Charlotte of her own awkwardness, especially since she was now unable to use her right hand.

"I have something to tell you," he said once Laura was out of sight.

Charlotte braced herself. She didn't want to hear how he felt about Laura. She waited. After several agonizing seconds, he revealed his news.

"I'm not going back to the island. I'm going to work for Mr. Ducharme for a while."

He was staying here. With Laura. To live happily ever after. A knife twisted in Charlotte's stomach.

Seth continued. "After a few weeks, I'm moving to Detroit. Mr. Garrity offered me a permanent job there with the Michigan Stove Company."

"You are? He did? Seth, that's wonderful! I mean I'll miss you. South Manitou Island won't be the same. But I'm glad you'll be in Detroit. I mean—"

"Charlie, listen to me a minute."

"Yes, Seth. I'm listening."

"Charlie, you know how I feel about you. You're very special to me. Now I want you to promise me three things. First, that you'll behave yourself. You know how easily you get into mischief. I won't be there to get you out. Second, promise me that you'll study hard. You're a very intelligent young lady. You'll go far with your teacher's help. Third, promise me that you'll write. Often."

"I promise, I promise, I promise!"

He reached across the table and squeezed her left hand. There was a smile on his face now that made him look almost like the old Seth again. "Good. I feel much better about things." He pulled a paper from his pocket. "Here's my address for the next few weeks. It's best you write to me in care of Laura's folks until I find my own place—as soon as your hand heals enough to pick up a pen, that is."

Charlie read the address, another home on Lakeshore Drive, before folding the paper and slipping it into her skirt pocket.

As if on cue, Laura returned, setting a full plate of fancy biscuits in the center of the table, then refilling each of their glasses. Their conversation continued until Seth suggested they should be on their way and let Charlie get a good night's sleep before her morning departure. They went inside and thanked Mercy Spencer for her hospitality. Seth retrieved his straw hat, and Laura her lace gloves, then Charlotte walked out on the veranda with them to say her final good-byes.

Laura offered her left hand, conscious of the tenderness that would prevent Charlotte from shaking with her right. Reluctantly, Charlotte accepted. "Good-bye, Charlotte. It's been a pleasure knowing you."

Charlotte simply nodded. She couldn't fault the girl for the sincerity in her voice.

Laura stepped off the porch, drifting in the direction of the carriage and driver waiting at the curb.

Seth stepped nearer Charlotte. Taking care not to brush against her right hand, he drew her so close she could smell his slightly spicy skin bracer, and see where he had missed a few fuzzy whiskers on his chin when shaving.

He pressed her cheek against his chest and whispered, "I'm going to miss you, Charlie. I'm going to miss you very much." He kissed her cheek near her ear, stirring strange and wonderful feelings inside her, confusing her. She didn't know what was happening, and couldn't understand why things seemed different with Seth tonight than they ever had before.

Maybe it wasn't Seth. Maybe it was merely her burns that made her feel awkward, always struggling to hold her right hand out of the way as she was doing now.

Even before he was ready to release her, she stepped out of his embrace. "When do you suppose you'll come back to South Manitou, Seth?"

There was a nervous edge to the question he had been hoping she would not ask. He looked down, scraping the toe of his highly polished shoe along a groove in the porch, then lifted his eyes to her once more. "I don't know. Mr. Garrity says I'll be too busy to come back for a good long while. Good-bye, Charlie."

She watched as he walked back to Laura. Charlotte's spirits sank as he took the other girl's hand to help her into the cabriolet. There was a certain flair about him, an elegance of movement she had never noticed before they left the island.

Laura said something and they laughed together. The sound of their mirth pierced straight through Charlotte's heart.

Maybe I'll never see him again! she thought with a start. *Maybe he'll marry Laura!*

She pulled Ducharmes' address from her pocket. With a new purpose, she went inside and climbed the staircase to her room. She had no intention of letting Seth—-or Laura—forget her easily. Burns or no, before she left Chicago, she would post a letter.

CHAPTER 14

South Manitou Island
May 1894

Charlotte hurried along the beach until she came to her favorite log, then sat down, pulled Seth's latest letter from her pocket, and carefully pried it open.

> *Dear Charlie,*
> *Good news! I am to return to South Manitou next month for your graduation! Mr. Garrity will be sailing that way and has offered to bring me.*
> *It will be so wonderful to see you again . . .*

Charlotte ran all the way home to tell Aurora the news. The graduation dress her sister was planning to make for her would have to be extra special, since Seth was coming back to the island for the first time since the Fair!

June 1894

Seth carried his small bag upstairs to the tiny bedroom he

had once shared with Nat. It didn't seem possible that the place had been empty for almost a year—ever since Nat had signed as crewman on a steamer last summer.

Seth could only stay the night—long enough to see Charlie graduate, and attend the party for her afterward, then he must be off again with Garrity to Chicago on business. Of course, Laura Ducharme would make the stay there pleasant. George was even starting to tease him about having a girl in each port. Seth had only laughed. He had learned that sometimes, what a fellow *didn't* say was as important as what he *did* say.

He adjusted his collar, straightened his tie, and took a clothes brush to his pinstripe suit. From his bag, he removed a tiny black velvet box, popped it open one last time to look at the gift he had bought Charlie, then snapped it shut and tucked it in his inside breast pocket.

Across the hall, he could hear Charlie's and Aurora's voices as they helped one another dress for the commencement. He checked his watch, then slipped it back into his vest pocket. Graduation exercises would begin in less than an hour. The girls would be ready soon.

He sat on his bunk, listening, waiting, looking out the window at a view he had missed far too long—the tower and the lake, the sun-dappled trees and the clean skies. He wanted to memorize it once more to take back with him to his tiny flat in Detroit. How often he had sat there in his lonely room and daydreamed of Charlie and South Manitou.

Mr. Garrity's stove works on the Detroit River seemed a world away. It *was* a world away, with the responsibility of seeing that shipments were loaded properly at the docks, and late nights in his boss's office, learning the inner workings of the company.

He was thankful for his job at the plant when the lakes were closed for shipping. He was even more thankful for the cruises on the yacht, and all that Stokes was teaching him about being an engineer on a steamer, but he was *most* thankful for the paycheck he received each week. At a time when Mr. Garrity had let several men go due to slackening sales and rough times, he had kept Seth on and even given him a pay increase. Long gone were the days of a year ago when he first hired on to the *Martha G.* for a week's stint at a dollar and a quarter a day plus bonus. He chuckled to himself at the thought. Little had he known then that in due time Mr. Garrity would be planning to one day make him a partner in his firm.

Living frugally as he was, he managed to put a decent portion of his pay into a savings account each week. It was his investment for the future.

The unlatching of Charlie's bedroom door interrupted his thoughts. Quickly he stepped into the hallway.

The first moment he saw her seemed suspended in time. The past year had matured her from a skinny little kid to a blossoming young lady. She had curves now where she'd never had them before, and her face appeared more oval in shape, with subtly sculpted cheekbones. Her hair was different, too, no longer hanging down on her shoulders, but wrapped into a knot at the back, with little curls along her forehead.

She was like a butterfly emerging from its cocoon—a beauty waiting to unfold with time. He cleared his throat, suddenly aware that he had been staring, and put on a grin.

From the instant Charlotte saw Seth, she felt self-conscious. She wasn't accustomed to the way the small train of her dress flowed behind her, touching the floor, nor the corset Aurora had convinced her was necessary to achieve the hourglass figure. Though she liked the manner in which the foundation garment defined her waistline, it pressed so hard against her ribs that she wondered whether she would have to give up breathing! And the puffy sleeves that she had longed to wear seemed like big balloons above her elbows. No wonder Seth was looking at her so strangely!

Then he offered his smile, showing the familiar crooked grin! It was so wonderful to see him again!

Despite the warmth of his smile, other things about him had changed. He had filled out some. His shoulders were broader, his chest larger, making him appear more rugged, while at the same time, the expensive blue pinstripe suit that so perfectly fit his expanded frame projected the image of a successful businessman.

Seth stepped forward. "Hello, Charlie. You look very nice."

The quiet, mellow voice, and his nearness made her feel like jelly inside, and she couldn't withhold a nervous giggle. "Thank you. So do you." Another giggle slipped out before she regained control of herself. "I'm glad you're back, Seth. How long can you stay?"

"Only until tomorrow," he said quickly, as if to forestall any plans that might include him, "then I'm off to Chicago. Mr. Garrity has business there."

Disappointment tempered the joy Charlotte had felt a moment earlier. "I suppose you'll be seeing Laura Ducharme again," she concluded with a stab of jealousy.

Seth let the comment pass, slipping the velvet box from his pocket. "Congratulations, Charlie. I never had any doubt you'd graduate at the top of your class."

Thoughts of Chicago and Laura Ducharme vanished as

Charlotte held the box in both hands, cradling its softness. Seth had paid a pretty penny for its contents, no doubt. Slowly, she lifted the lid, which bore the name of a Detroit jeweler inside. Beneath it, on a black velvet pillow, lay a chased gold locket with one tiny bright diamond at the center of the oval, and a raised, leaf-like border around the edges. The gift was even more extravagant than she had anticipated. She chose her words carefully. "Seth Trevelyn, if you hadn't brought this all the way from Detroit, and if I didn't like it so much, I'd send you right back to the store with it and make you exchange it for something less expensive."

He couldn't help laughing. She reminded him of the Charlie he had always known. "It wouldn't do you a bit of good, young lady. That's the one I chose for you, and that's the one you keep!"

She removed the delicate chain from the velvet-covered card that held it in place, and handed it to him. "In that case, you had better help me put it on so everyone who sees me tonight can appreciate it."

Suddenly, Seth was all fumble-fingers. His hands seemed to tremble uncontrollably. He was glad Charlie's back was to him. She would surely notice his jitters, then issue a barrage of teasing questions he was not prepared to answer. After a few moments, he managed to open the clasp, then fasten it around her neck.

She stepped into her room to set the velvet box on her dresser, then returned to face him again. The locket lay nestled in the ruffles of her bodice. She lifted it and pried it open. Two strangers stared back at her---the jewelers models advertising the locket. Someday, she would replace those pictures with others that had real meaning.

From downstairs, her mother's voice drifted up to her.

"Charlotte? Are you ready? We'd better go."

"Coming, Mama."

She snapped the locket shut. Her eyes met Seth's hazel ones, so full of tenderness and admiration. She reached up, taking his face in her hands and rising onto her toes.

He steadied her, his hands at her waist, and when her eyes drifted shut, he bent to her waiting lips, the essence of her rosewater surrounding him.

The brief, exquisite kiss set Charlotte spinning. Though she had come down off her toes once more, she thought she would surely lose her balance, and leaned against him, the mild spiciness of his skin bracer encircling her.

His arms went around her in a gentle embrace. It lasted no more than a few precious seconds. Then, as if of one mind, they turned to descend the stairs, Charlotte's hand on his steady arm as she sought to recover her equilibrium.

A week after graduation, Charlotte was alone on the balcony of the lighthouse, taking pleasure in the sight of a schooner, white sails billowing, as it moved slowly through the passage. Memories of Seth's recent visit were still vivid, especially the kiss and embrace they had shared when he had given her his gift. They would remain in her mind always. She wondered if they would remain in Seth's, or had Laura Ducharme chased them away with her light-hearted manner and *Harper's Bazar* fashions?

Charlotte looked down at the pendant she had not taken off since he had fastened it about her neck. She opened it and studied the anonymous faces—a young woman who would command second looks from any young man, and a fellow dashing enough to deserve her. The thought occurred to her that she hadn't looked beneath the store pictures. With her fingernail, she pried out the image of the young woman. Much to her surprise, an engraving hid underneath.

CHAPTER 15

Charlotte wasted no time in lifting out the photograph of the young man that occupied the right half of the locket. For a minute or two, she stared at the message engraved in the gold.

To	*Love,*
C.	*S.*

Carefully, she replaced the miniature portraits. Already, she had suffered teasing enough over the fact that Seth had given her the locket, so she had shown the anonymous photographs to everyone who'd had the audacity to suggest she was carrying Seth's picture inside. The engraving would remain her secret and hers alone.

More troubling were the feelings that had stirred inside her on graduation night when he had kissed her and held her. She would never forget the tingly sensation. It came to her each time she relived the affectionate moments.

She missed Seth terribly. Why did he have to live so far away? Why couldn't he visit more often?

At least if she could not be with him, she could put her time to good use pursuing her high school diploma with Mrs. Garrity's guidance.

June 1896

Seth adjusted the brim of his straw hat against the sun as he leaned into the stern rail, watching the sandy island with its tiny white dot in the distance. He filled his lungs with clean air that smelled like nothing in particular, purified by the northern lake waters over which it had blown. Its coolness tempered the warmth of the brilliant sun, bringing comfort.

As the *Martha G.* made her way through the Manitou Passage, the white speck on Sandy Point gradually grew until it was distinguishable as the South Manitou light tower, tall and proud, elegant and stately, welcoming Seth home. George let off several blasts of his steam whistle before he entered the harbor and positioned himself in line behind two steamers for a place at the dock at South Manitou.

The wait gave Seth an opportunity to study the familiar island. Its beautiful sandy beach, lovely trees, and clear air stirred him. They couldn't be more different from the paved, bustling, often foul-smelling city he had left behind. The curved arms of the bay seemed to embrace him, offering a comfortable haven from the sticky heat of Chicago where George had just completed a new deal with Ducharme.

He checked his timepiece. Charlotte would still be at school helping Mrs. Garrity. After the *Martha G.* was tied up, he would head over there and walk her home.

His nerves went taut. Despite the fact that he hadn't

seen Charlotte for two years, and their correspondence had trickled off to an exchange of cordial letters every couple of months, she was never far from his mind.

He wondered how she had changed since her graduation from eighth grade. She had been but a fourteen-year-old then. Now she was a mature sixteen-year-old on the brink of womanhood. It was just as well George had kept him so busy in the years while he was waiting for her to grow up, that he hadn't been able to spend much time coming back to visit. He had learned the last time he had come to see Charlotte that when it came time for him to go, he hated leaving her behind.

Helen stooped to pick up a scrap of paper from beneath the desk, and pressed her hand to the painful small of her back as she straightened, thankful that the school day was over. She was reminded by the ache how much she had come to depend upon Charlie for such routine tasks. Her young assistant had made a habit of cleaning up the schoolroom every night, but word had come a few minutes ago that the *Martha G.* was in port, and she had insisted Charlie go and welcome Seth home for his first visit since her graduation two years ago.

Returning to the front of the room, Helen tossed the paper scrap into the wastebasket, took a deep breath, and let it out slowly. The news that George was in port had set her on edge. Though he had written from time to time, she hadn't answered his letters, and she hadn't seen him since he had brought Seth to the island for Charlie's graduation. That brief encounter had proved awkward, for each of them had been preoccupied—she with the graduation exercises, he with difficult business transactions to be negotiated two days later in Chicago.

She hoped he was only in port for a few hours, too brief a time to look her up. Maybe he would stay on his yacht. Avoidance was easier than facing his groping questions, and reckoning with her own uncertain feelings.

She went to the flip chart in the corner and began turning back the pages to the beginning, trying to put her mind on other topics. Another school year completed, her fourth since coming to the island in the fall of 1892. It hardly seemed possible, time had passed so quickly.

When she turned around to make one final inspection of her schoolroom, there was George, watching her from the doorway at the back. Her pulse fluttered as he stepped forward.

"Hello, Helen. Miss Richards told me I'd find you here. It's good to see you again."

He was perceptibly more relaxed than the last time she had seen him. A grin separated his thick mustache from his neatly trimmed beard. Under his left arm he held a box tied with a wide satin ribbon. With his free hand, he removed his commodore's cap, tucked it, too, beneath his arm, and ran his fingers through his unruly thick brown hair.

"Hello, George. I see fair winds have once again blown you into our harbor. It's been so long, I'd almost forgotten what you looked like."

Her modest smile bolstered his courage, which had been badly flagging in anticipation of this long overdue visit. Seeing the lights dancing in her blue eyes, he wondered how he had let business get in the way of his pursuit of her. Like a good wine, she had improved with age. Her petite figure was still in perfect trim, and the strands of gray that now salted her curly bangs made her even more attractive than before.

One thing hadn't changed though. She was dressed as severely as she had been two years ago, in a plain white blouse and unremarkable dark skirt.

As she approached him, she noticed that his coat, stretching at the buttons the last time she had seen him, now closed comfortably over a less obvious paunch. With the weight loss, he was cutting a more handsome figure than before.

One thing hadn't changed. He still indulged his cigars, for she could smell the stale smoke clinging to his suit when she had come to stand within an arm's length of him.

George scanned the room briefly, then his eyes rested on her once more. "How about closing up this place and letting me walk you home?"

Helen nodded. "I'll get my things."

On the half-mile walk to her home, George talked of his business, and how it was beginning to improve after the downturn following the closing of the World's Columbian Exposition of '93.

It seemed good to be with him again, to hear his voice. It was a gruffer version of Robert's, but the brotherly similarity was nevertheless evident, and in a way, comforting.

Once inside her modest cottage, she offered him her most comfortable cushioned wicker chair, kindled a fire in her kitchen stove to heat water for tea, then sat across from him, separated by a white wicker table which now held the beribboned box he had brought.

He shoved the parcel toward her. "Go on. Open it," he urged, a gleam of anticipation in his eyes.

"After your long absence, did you think you would have to buy your way back into my good graces with a gift?" she half-teased.

He offered a sheepish grin. "You know me too well."

She contemplated the box a moment, then pushed it back toward George. "I really can't accept this. It would be just as well if you returned it to the store and got your money back."

"Too late now. It can't be returned, so you'll just have to keep it." He slid it toward her again. When she made no move to touch it, he picked it up. "All right, be stubborn. I'll open it for you." With a flamboyant tug, he whipped off the huge rose-colored satin ribbon then flung off the lid. Flipping back the tissue, he held up a white silk vest and a large cravat of white chiffon, part of a stylish Paris ensemble.

Helen caught her breath at the beauty of the double-breasted style with its two rows of shiny gold buttons. "George, what on earth has gotten into you? You know this is too fancy—"

"You're wrong about that! Now be still and let me show you the rest of the costume!" He laid the vest and cravat aside and held up a short coat with a cut-away front in grayish-green silk, and the matching godet-shaped skirt, its front pleats caught with a series of green velvet knots, each adorned by a fancy button.

It was absolutely the most extravagant, expensive, stylish suit Helen had ever seen. She ran her fingers over the large-branched broché design of the material. "You realize I could never wear this suit," she said, a hint of regret in her voice.

"Don't be silly. You'd look stunning in it. Go try it on." He draped the skirt and jacket across her lap, adding to them the vest and cravat.

She admired them a moment, then began putting them back in the box. "It's far too ostentatious for South Manitou Island," she concluded.

He leaned forward, hands on knees. "Then come off the island with me," he urged. "Move back to the mainland. I'll show you plenty of places where it will fit right in, starting with Mackinac Island. I'm going there for a week's vacation. Come with me. I have a room reserved for you at Grand Hotel."

She couldn't miss the intensity in his gray eyes. She looked down, pondering the garment on which he had spent lavishly, then smoothed the tissue over it and set the lid in place. "I can't leave here, George. I have commitments to fulfill. Charlie is taking her exams this week. She's only halfway through her high school courses and—"

"She's not your daughter," he brusquely reminded her.

"But she's given me a real purpose," Helen quickly countered. "I felt so lost when Robert died . . . "

George remembered how distraught Helen had been when he had first brought her here. Thankfully, those days had passed long ago. Now, there were other issues to face. "Miss Richards will leave here someday. Then what will you do?" he asked, not unkindly.

"There will be other students who need me," she replied. "Now, if you'll excuse me, I'll go make tea. I'm sure the water is boiling by now." As she rose, she started to set the box on the table.

"Oh, no, you don't, Helen. You're not casting aside my gift so easily!" Grinning broadly, he put one hand on the box, one hand about her waist, and forced her in the direction of the bedroom off the parlor. "I'll see to the tea. You're going to try this on."

"But, George—"

"No buts! I'm not leaving until you walk out here wearing my gift!" He gently shoved her across the threshold and closed the door firmly between them.

After several minutes of puttering about the kitchen, George managed to locate Helen's teapot and tea leaves, cups, saucers, and spoons, and a tray on which to carry it all to the little wicker table in the parlor. He had put everything in readiness and was leaning back in the padded wicker chair when Helen's door opened.

CHAPTER 16

The moment Helen stepped out of her bedroom, George knew the suit had been meant for her, just as his intuition had told him when he had first discovered it in the French seamstress's window. Seeing it on Helen now, made it worth every penny of the exorbitant price the mademoiselle had extracted. And just as the woman had told him, the cravat draping the bust added the perfect finishing touch.

In keeping with the suit's stylish mode, Helen had rearranged her naturally wavy hair, drawing it back more loosely in a becoming coiffure. The way she looked now, he could easily imagine her standing at his side before a minister, exchanging marriage vows, but he was certain those thoughts were far from her mind.

Though Helen had thought trying on the suit was a waste of time, the pleased look on George's face made the exercise worthwhile. The design was considerably fancier than even her own wedding dress had been, one she had chosen for its practicality when marrying a doctoral student facing heavy educational expenses.

She had not thought then that her marriage would be so brief, nor that one day her brother-in-law would be presenting her with gifts which would obligate her to his further attentions. The fact that she neither wanted to hurt him nor be pressured by him, made her dilemma all the more vexing.

George came to her, offering his arm as if to escort her to some grand occasion. "If I do say so myself, Helen, I have managed to exercise magnificent taste in both women and fashion. You should wear suits like this more often. You look absolutely ravishing!"

"Thank you, George, but high fashion has no real place on the island. I have no intention of keeping it."

"No need to decide now. Come. Let's have tea and I'll tell you the news from Detroit."

Unaccustomed to the fluffy cravat at her throat and the balloon-like sleeves that flared out from her shoulders, Helen sipped tea twice as strong as she herself would have brewed, and listened to George tell of the improving outlook for both his stove company in Detroit and the refrigeration business he partnered with Ducharme in Chicago.

No wonder George hadn't succeeded in impressing lady friends. Business seemed the only area he was able to converse in at any length!

Hearing him now, Helen realized it was a topic that had never put her off, and she was glad to let him dominate the conversation. He had been doing so for an hour when he suddenly put down his teacup and checked his pocket watch. "It's nearly dinner time. What do you say to some wonderful French cuisine on the *Martha G.*? Mother hired a new chef who has mastered the art of creating sauces."

Reluctantly, Helen set her own teacup on the tray. Her answer would indicate far more than her response to a dinner invitation. It would set the course for the immediate future of their relationship. She considered the prospect carefully before responding. "I think not, George, but thank you for inviting me. Now, if you'll excuse me, I'll go change. You really must return this suit to the store."

"Not a chance," he said, rising with her.

"But it's not at all my style," she argued. "I feel terribly self-conscious in something so showy."

"Then keep it and wear it in private until you feel comfortable enough to step out in it," he insisted.

She would have argued further, but he pressed a finger to her lips. "I'll hear no more about it. Now, if you won't come with me to my yacht, at least see me out."

Though it was a struggle, Helen maintained her silence while the swish of silk accompanied them to the door.

George faced her, taking each of her hands in his. "You know, Helen, you can't hide away on this island forever. One of these days, I'll be back for you, and I won't take no for an answer." He kissed the back of each of her hands, then let himself out.

The screen door squeaked shut, and she watched from behind it as he walked down the path. As he disappeared from sight, she tried to sort out the myriad of feelings stirring inside her—the knowledge that George would make a very fine, caring husband, should a woman be inclined to marry, the need she felt to continue working with Charlie and the other students, and her desire to remain cloistered in the shelter of this island.

Would she ever feel safe leaving this haven, stepping back into the mainstream of life?

Clutching her history book to her breast, Charlotte put aside concerns over the final examination she would take tomorrow, and stepped briskly along the dock toward the *Martha G.*, nervous over the prospect of seeing Seth for the first time in two years. George Garrity had already come off his yacht, remarked about the fine sailing weather he'd had coming from Chicago, inquired about his sister-in-law, and sent Charlotte on her way with assurances that Seth would soon follow.

She was still several yards away when his lanky figure appeared on deck. With satchel in hand, he descended the gangway and turned toward her, waving the moment he spotted her.

She caught her breath at the sight of him. He was not in a suit as he had been the last several times she'd seen him. He wore a blue cotton work shirt and denim pants, reminding her of the casual days of their childhood, except he'd grown so very handsome! Her heart told her to run to greet him, but her knees turned to sponges.

The instant Seth recognized Charlie, he wanted only to hurry to her and scoop her into his arms, holding her tight! But too much time had passed since his last visit, and his inner voice cautioned restraint. As she came closer, he realized that the young butterfly he had seen at eighth grade graduation had now unfolded her wings, and a beautiful creature she was, despite the simple style of her yellow shirtwaist and navy skirt. Cautious as a swallowtail in flight, she came toward him.

He made no effort to speak while taking in her toffee-colored hair, swept up onto the top of her head, her clear brown eyes sparkling with topaz highlights, and her generous mouth that offered a smile. Memories came flooding back of what it had been like to kiss her, making him want to taste her sweet lips again, but such affections must wait.

Charlotte could hardly believe Seth was here, standing before her! His amber brown hair had receded a little since she had last seen him, but his lopsided grin hadn't changed. His greenish-brown eyes twinkled with some unspoken pleasure—was he really glad to see her?

Feelings that had long been tucked into the tiniest corner of her heart were now set free, causing it to flutter. With her left hand, she gripped her book more tightly in an effort to calm herself. With her right, she reached out, intertwining her slender fingers with his strong ones.

"Welcome home, Seth. I'm awfully glad you're here."

As Seth wrapped his fingers about her small hand, he realized how badly he wanted never to let go. "And I'm glad to be here, Charlie. It's wonderful to see you again."

His response constituted a masterpiece of understatement. He silently vowed to spend the coming week— his first week of vacation in three years—convincing her how much he cared about her.

Walking off the dock with Charlotte at his side, he wanted only to be alone with her, but islanders whom he hadn't seen in two years recognized him and greeted him, leading to long-overdue chats which he tried to keep as brief as possible. He clutched Charlie's hand tightly while he talked—with Tom Foster, the postmaster, who probably knew the exact number of letters he had written to Charlie since his last visit, and Otto Schroeder, in town to pick up a new piece of farm equipment that had been delivered from

Chicago.

Schroeder seemed a bit standoffish, and Seth was reminded of news he'd had from his older brother, Nat, a few weeks ago. He waited until he and Charlotte had walked several yards down the beach toward home, away from the bustle at the dock, and their conversation had advanced from nervous small talk about weather to more comfortable exchanges about family, to raise the subject that had long been on his mind.

"I got a letter from Nat last month," he began. "He said he and Meta Schroeder had eloped the last time he was up this way. I knew he'd been sweet on her for a long time, but I was kind of expecting to be invited to the wedding."

Charlotte understood Seth's disappointment. Meta had been her best friend until they had finished grammar school. Since then, they had drifted apart, but Charlotte, too, had been hurt to learn of the secret marriage. "I don't suppose Nat and Meta wanted to wait until they could plan a regular wedding. With the island lacking a minister, it was just simpler to sail across to Glen Arbor," she reasoned, telling only part of what she knew.

"I suppose a formal wedding isn't as important as happiness," Seth surmised. "Nat said now that he's married, he's never been more content. I presume Meta feels the same."

"She seemed happy enough the last time I saw her," Charlotte allowed. Impatient to turn to other topics, she held out her history text. "Tomorrow, I have to know everything in this book for my final exam. Do you suppose you could help me study after supper?"

Seth squeezed her hand. "Sure. We'll take it over to the small lake where it's quiet and we won't be interrupted," he suggested, knowing full well that while Charlie was studying history, he'd be studying her.

Seth spread a blanket on the grassy shore of the inland lake for Charlie. She sat down, and he lowered himself beside her, realizing it had been years since he'd visited this spot. For a few moments, his attention was captured by the natural beauty of this wilderness refuge—the great blue heron feeding on the fish, the common loons swimming several yards from shore, their haunting calls echoing off the still surface of the water. Above, nighthawks circled, their nasal *peent, peent, peent* overpowering the bullfrog and cricket symphony below.

At his side, Charlie was absorbed in her history book. Gently, he reached up to brush a stray tendril from her cheek. Unconsciously, it seemed, she pushed his hand away while turning back the pages in the book.

Having Seth so near was disconcerting to Charlotte. She couldn't focus on the words in her book. It didn't matter at the moment what had caused the panic of 1873, nor why many Republicans had voted with the Democrats in 1876. His gentle touch was enough to make her want to melt against him.

But tomorrow, she would be sitting in the schoolhouse, and Mrs. Garrity would hand her a blue book and a page of questions. Then, she would regret time wasted this evening. She turned to the first chapter of the text and handed it to Seth. "We might as well start at the beginning. That's the part I'm having the most trouble remembering. We've got to cover as much as possible before it's too dark to read."

Reluctantly, Seth took up the book. He began with the

questions following the first chapter, about differences in savage, barbarous, and half-civilized Indians, and proceeded through the colonization of North America, the Revolution, and the Federal union, barely able to make out the words by the time he reached the last two questions.

"What was the object of the Columbian Fair, and why was it remarkable?"

"That's easy. The Fair commemorated the discovery of America by Christopher Columbus, and was remarkable because of the architectural beauty and artistic grouping of its buildings." Charlotte paused, then chuckled. "Mrs. Garrity would never forgive me if I got that wrong, after all the trouble she went to, taking me to Chicago with her." She rose, shaking out her skirt. "It's getting dark fast. We'd better get back."

Though Seth would have preferred staying there in the dark with Charlie, he got up, folded the blanket, and draped it over his shoulder. They started down the path toward the lighthouse, his hand at the small of her back.

The slightest touch from Seth made Charlotte want to forget everything else. But she couldn't afford to forget about history until her exam was finished. She stepped ahead, chattering over her shoulder. "Thanks for your help, Seth. I feel much better about tomorrow. I couldn't bear to do poorly and disappoint Mrs. Garrity after all the time she's spent going over history lessons with me."

Seth lengthened his stride, catching up with her, but this time, he kept his hand to himself. "Charlie, how would you like to go fishing with me after your test tomorrow? I have this whole week off while Mr. Garrity visits Mackinac Island. The Ducharmes are meeting him up there. That leaves me free for seven days of fun. We can go fishing every day, if we want to!"

The mention of Ducharmes brought Laura to mind. She wondered whether Seth had seen Miss *Harper's Bazar* while in Chicago, but was not about to ask. Seth was here now, and she would make the most of it. "I'll go fishing if you'll promise to help me study for the English test Mrs. Garrity is giving me the day after tomorrow. The day after that, I have my Mathematics exam. Then I'll be able to forget about school."

"It's not exactly what I had in mind, but I'll help you," he promised, adding, "Charlie, when we get back to the keeper's quarters, would you like to sit on the beach for a while and talk? It would be nice to discuss something besides school work."

Charlotte laughed. "I suppose we could, but just for a little while. I have to get a good night's rest so I'll be fresh in the morning."

The sky was fully dark by the time they reached home, except for the light from the tower that sent its steady white beam across the rippling waters of the passage. While Charlie went inside to put her book away, Seth found a sandy place on the beach where he spread the blanket. Then he sat down to wait, thinking about the things he wanted to say to her—important things he'd never told her before—things that, seeing her now, he realized he couldn't keep locked in his heart any longer. He was still organizing his thoughts when she joined him a few minutes later, taking a place on the far edge of the blanket.

The tower threw just enough light behind her to profile her head, with the straight nose, and the slight downturn to her pretty mouth. "I hope I do well on that test tomorrow," she fretted. "Mrs. Garrity—"

"Charlie, I thought we agreed to talk about something else," he gently reminded her.

She put her hand to her forehead. "There I go, discussing school work again. I'm sorry. What was it you wanted to talk about?"

In the silent moments that followed, she studied the way the light reflected off the solid shoulders of the man beside her, and played on the angles of his cheekbones. She fought the desire to move closer, within reach of his strong arms.

After some consideration, Seth decided to approach the subject head on. Quietly, he told her, "I wanted to talk about us, Charlie. I've missed you. More than you know."

His admission threatened to weaken her resolve, but she remained steadfastly in place. "And I've missed you, Seth," she half-whispered.

"I can't describe how great it is to be home again," he said, moving closer. He reached out, capturing her hand in his. "This island is wonderful because of you, Charlie. I love you. I want to marry you."

His words stunned her. She could barely think. As much as she cared about Seth, she simply wasn't prepared. Drawing a shallow breath, she spoke quietly. "I hardly know what to say to you."

Even in the dim light of the tower, he could see the troubled look in her eyes. "Say you'll marry me, Charlie."

"But—"

"We could get married on Saturday, then you could come with me on the *Martha G.*, and move into my flat in Detroit." His plans spilled out in a rush. "I don't want to leave here without you, Charlie. We'd be so happy, like Nat and Meta!"

Charlotte pulled her hand from Seth's and stiffened. "Like Nat and Meta?" she said incredulously. "But they got married because they *had* to!"

Seth was shocked by the news. "What?"

"She's going to have a baby six months from now. Theirs was hardly a romantic wedding, sneaking off like they did. Meta was too scared to tell her folks until they were hitched. With Nat away so much, her life is little different from when she was single. She still lives with her parents when Nat's not here. When he comes home, they stay in a tiny little place her papa put up at the edge of one of his meadows. It's awful, Seth! Just awful!"

"It'll be much better for us," he argued. "You've got a whole week to plan. And everybody knows you wouldn't be marrying me because you had to!"

Charlotte got to her feet. Seth did, too, and she faced him squarely, looking up at the man who stood nearly a foot taller than she. "I love you, Seth, but I'm not ready to marry you. Not this week. Not this year. What about my high school diploma? I have two years of study ahead of me. I couldn't *possibly* get married now. It would be *such* a disappointment to Mrs. Garrity." She turned to walk away, but Seth stopped her, his hand on her arm.

"Mrs. Garrity this, Mrs. Garrity that! For years, it seems all I've heard about is Mrs. Garrity! I'm sick of it! I should have proposed to Laura Ducharme when I was in Chicago this week. She would have said yes in an instant, and she never talks about Mrs. Garrity!"

Charlotte wrenched her arm free. "I'm sorry you feel the way you do! It seems to me, if you really loved me like you say, you'd wait till I'd finished my schooling. If you can't, then be on your way to Laura!" Charlotte could no longer hold back her tears, and they spilled down her cheeks. "Now you've got me so upset, I'll never pass my history test tomorrow!" She turned and ran to the keeper's quarters.

Charlotte hurried up the front stairs to her room, thankful that neither of her sisters were in to see her sobbing. She closed the door behind her, despite the warmth of the still summer night.

She listened for Seth to come up the stairs to his room across the hall, agonizing over the choice she had made, and the things that had been said about Laura. She went to bed and lay wide awake, wondering whether Seth really would marry the rich city girl.

She heard footsteps on the stairs two hours later, but they were not Seth's. Aurora and Bridget were coming to bed. Charlotte pretended to be asleep, listening while her sisters whispered to one another about Seth and his abrupt change of plans to stay on the *Martha G.* tonight, and go on to Mackinac Island with George Garrity in the morning for a week's vacation at Grand Hotel.

While he was living in the lap of luxury, Charlotte would be studying, and nursing a heart so bruised she wondered whether it would ever heal.

CHAPTER
17

September 1898

As George walked the path from the dock to Helen's cottage, he realized it had been weeks since he had felt an urge this strong to light a cigar. He had resisted it then, and he would resist it now. He had no intention of lapsing back into his old habit. It had been difficult enough to quit smoking in the first place. He had no need to relive the agony, regardless of the fact that he was more edgy than he had been in years, coming to see Helen, his heart in his hand, to settle the issue once and for all of her leaving South Manitou.

But for all his nervousness, when he arrived at Helen's cottage, he found it closed up tight, and realized he had erred in judgment once again where the dedicated teacher was concerned. At five in the afternoon, he had thought she would have long since left the schoolhouse. Surely she would be home soon.

Too fidgety to sit on the front stoop and wait, he let himself in. That was one of the advantages of living on the fringe of civilization, he supposed. One could leave doors and windows unlocked without fear that a thief or vandal would enter in one's absence.

The rose potpourri-scented air in the cottage was close. The skies had been dark, threatening rain early that morning. She had obviously considered the weather before going to school, and had closed every window tight. Instead of precipitation, the clouds and warm southern breezes had brought uncomfortably high levels of heat and humidity. He went from window to window, opening them to air the place out—first the two parlor windows, then the kitchen window, but there was little cross ventilation from the north and east. He mopped his brow and paused at Helen's half-open bedroom door. The windows facing the south and west were in her room. He was reluctant to enter it, but the place would never cool down unless he opened those windows, too. After a moment's consideration, he pushed the door fully open and entered the small room.

He felt like an invader, allowing himself into Helen's most private quarters, but he reasoned that it was as necessary for her good as his that the cottage be a comfortable place in which to take an evening meal after a day's work. When he had opened the two windows, he lingered. On her dresser was the Staffordshire porcelain hair receiver his mother had given Helen years ago. It had belonged to his maternal grandmother, and Helen had put it to good use, saving the brown silk strands she had salvaged from her silver-backed brush.

Her boudoir was almost as tidy as the rest of the place.

The wardrobe doors were latched shut, not left ajar with clothes spilling out as was often the case with his own. On top of the tall oak piece was a large department store box. He recognized it immediately. It was the same box he had brought to Helen the last time he had come to the island, a little over two years ago. He couldn't help taking it down to look inside. When he removed the lid, he found the white silk vest and gray-green suit, just as it looked on the day he had given it to her. He couldn't keep back a wry smile. He put the box away, and with the characteristic clumsiness that accompanied his nervous state, he knocked a stack of papers off her bedstand.

When he bent to pick them up, he discovered that she had kept all his correspondence through the years, though she hadn't answered any of it. The most recent letter he had sent her was on top. It lay open, as if she had recently been rereading it. He read again the lines he had penned to her last June.

Dearest Helen,

Another school year has come to an end for you. I do wish you would consider making it your last on the island and remedy one of the problems you have often urged me to solve, that of my need for a wife. You know I am very fond of you, Helen. I can give you a comfortable life here in Detroit. I am certain you care for me at least a little, or you would have put a stop to my attentions long ago.

I realize that you would have a difficult time finding a regular teaching position in this city once you remarry, but there are many students here who would benefit greatly from your private tutoring, and the house is set up with an office you could use for that purpose.

I understand your prize pupil will be attending the University of Michigan come fall, if what Seth tells me is to be believed. With Charlotte leaving the island, it seems like a good time for a change in your own life. I told you the last time I visited you, that one day I would come back, and I would not take no for an answer. That time is drawing ever nearer. Life holds many opportunities, and I do not intend allowing you to let them slip by.

These words are written from my heartfelt concern for you, Helen, and my genuine affection.

As ever,
George

P.S. I have recently attained the state of perfection. I have given up completely my nasty cigar habit. What more could you ask for? (Ha, ha!)

George laid the letter on top of the others and wandered back to the parlor. It had cooled down considerably with the island breeze now flowing through, but he was feeling too tense to rest in the padded wicker chair he had occupied on his previous visit. Besides, his stomach, which was much smaller now that he had managed to seriously cut back on the French sauces and pastries in which he had indulged too heavily for years, was beginning to complain. He doubted the feelings resulted from a natural appetite—rather they were likely caused by his anxiety. Nevertheless, he decided to take a look in the kitchen.

It had changed little since he had made tea there two years ago. Helen still had the same cookstove. On the counter she had set a green pepper and a few tomatoes from her garden. Dried herbs hung from a string draped from one corner to the other. He checked the onion bin, and the contents of the icebox and discovered everything necessary for omelettes with fried bacon. From a peg, he helped himself to her apron and tied it on, then kindled a fire in the stove, filled the coffeepot and set it on the burner. Assembling utensils and ingredients, he rolled up his shirt sleeves and set about putting into practice the cooking skills Pierre, the French chef he had hired two years ago, had taught him.

As he worked, he sang the French ditties Pierre had taught him and thought about some of the advice the chef had given George regarding women. He would keep it in mind tonight.

He was setting several strips of crisp bacon aside to drain when he saw Helen come in.

She had heard the singing as she came down the path, and had been surprised to find her door open. But she had been told that the *Martha G.* was in the harbor, and George was the only person in her acquaintance who would be brash enough to invite himself into her home in her absence.

Her heart beat erratically as the words of his last letter came to mind. She took a deep breath to calm herself, then opened the door. The aromas of coffee and fried bacon were a welcoming treat.

When she reached the kitchen doorway, she thought for one startling moment that she was looking at Robert. George's clean-shaven face and neatly combed hair made him look like an older version of his brother.

She had never seen him without his beard and mustache, and she required a moment to adjust to the shock. When she at last took notice of the rest of him, she realized how odd this tall, brawny man looked wearing her skimpy ruffled apron. The sight of him sent her into stitches!

George set down the bowl of eggs he had whipped to a frothy lemon yellow, half pleased, half embarrassed at the reaction he had drawn from Helen. He couldn't remember the last time he had seen her laugh so hard. Maybe she was beginning to loosen up—even if she hadn't altered her white-blouse-dark-skirt wardrobe. Her high-pitched trill was contagious, and soon he was chuckling, too.

Helen struggled to regain control of herself, dabbing the tears from her eyes. "Hello, George. I never expected to find you in my kitchen, nor in my apron!" She narrowly escaped lapsing into giggles again before she continued in a more serious tone. "Quite honestly, I didn't know your talents extended beyond tea."

George bent low to kiss her hand, straightening slowly in the continental style as Pierre had showed him. "Good evening, Ma'amoiselle. I make for you a most delightful omelette," he said, mimicking Pierre's accent. Her blue eyes sparkled like he had never seen before. Taking her by the elbow, he ushered her out of the kitchen. "Go. Refresh yourself while I finish my gastronomical delight."

"I have an even better idea. While you're completing your masterpiece, I'll set the table."

Helen couldn't keep from smiling to herself at the changes in George as she took her china and flatware from the corner hutch and set it out on her round oak table in the dining area of the parlor. From time to time, she glanced at him working at the stove. Beneath the ridiculous-looking apron, it was obvious he had lost considerable weight since their last parting, and the fact that cigar smoke no longer clung to his clothing was indeed a refreshing change.

She hardly knew what to make of the fact that he had taken over her kitchen in her absence. Two years ago, brewing tea had taxed his culinary skills beyond their limit. Now he was playing the role of a chef and quite obviously enjoying every minute.

She finished her table setting and stepped into her room to wash her face. When she saw that the windows were already open, a strange feeling came over her, knowing that George had been in her sleeping chamber. For a moment, she felt somehow violated, though reason told her he had only entered there with the most honorable intention of letting in cooling breezes.

A knock sounded on her door. "Supper is ready when you are."

"I'll be right out." She hung her towel on the bar, checked her hair in the mirror, and smoothed some unruly waves into place before joining him.

George held her chair, then took his place beside her. Crisp bacon, a tempting golden-brown omelette speckled with bits of green and red, and a sprig of parsley garnish filled Helen's plate, sending up a hint of subtle herb seasoning to tantalize her. She bowed her head briefly to say grace. When she looked up again, George was waiting anxiously for her reaction. She wasted no time cutting into the eggs, then savored the delectable blend of vegetables and herbs, nodding her head in approval before she finished swallowing.

"Since you wouldn't come to my yacht to partake of Pierre's cuisine, I decided to bring it to you," George explained.

"I'm very thankful you did," said Helen, taking another substantial bite accompanied by sounds of approval.

"If I'd known you were going to be this enthusiastic, I wouldn't have waited two years," George teased. Though he spoke lightly of the long interval since their last meeting, seeing Helen as relaxed as she was with him now, made him want more than ever to take her off the island.

As the dinner table talk moved through several topics including culinary skills, French impressionist painters, and their American counterparts, Helen realized George had changed as much on the inside as he had on the outside. In the first hour of conversation, the stove plant was never even mentioned. Not until the dishes had been cleared and they were seated comfortably beside one another on the parlor sofa, did their discussion turn away from the arts.

George waited until Helen had seemed completely at ease, taking her hand in his to broach the subject that had been foremost on his mind. "There's something I'd like to say, Helen, and it hasn't anything to do with the arts. It has to do with you and me. I'm not going to disguise it in clever euphemisms or romantic soliloquy. I'm going to be blunt." He looked straight into her blue eyes. She glanced down briefly, then returned his direct gaze. Though his heart was pumping harder than if he'd won a ten-mile cycle race at the sportsman's club, he continued. "Helen, I love you. I want to marry you. I want to take you with me when I leave this island."

George's declaration, though not unexpected, still sent a jolt of electricity through her. How she wanted to save them both an ocean of heartache and simply say yes, but that was impossible.

Her thoughts raced. If only she could tell him how close she had come to leaving South Manitou this past summer, how another teacher, one in whom she had confidence to do a good job, had nearly replaced her. But before that teacher had signed a contract, he was offered a better position.

And it was just as well, for the prospect of leaving the island for the challenges of the mainland had given her second thoughts. Being a good wife would take more effort than being a good teacher. It required a commitment, heart and soul, to one person. She had taken that kind of risk once. She didn't know if she would ever be ready to do so again.

She tried to free her hands from George's. She needed to be away from him a moment, to think of a way to respond, but he wouldn't let her go. She became very still, clearing her throat to say the three words that would suffice for all the rest.

"I can't go."

A muscle in George's jaw flinched, the only indication of what had to be for him a bitter disappointment. He released her, rising from the sofa to pace to the door, pausing there to stare out into the darkness before returning to sit beside her again, leaving several inches between them. "You're still keeping yourself in a box, Helen, just like the dress I brought you last time I came. When are you going to come out and start to live again?" He spoke with controlled anger.

She could think of no response.

"Two years ago, I said I wouldn't take no for an answer. I was wrong. You won't hear from me again." He thought a moment, then a derisive laugh escaped him.

"Mother was right. I fear you will pick up a crooked stick at the last, or perhaps no stick at all."

Without another word, he let himself out, the screen door creaking open, then slamming shut behind him.

CHAPTER 18

Charlotte set her brush and comb on the dresser in the Michigan Cabin aboard the *Martha G.*, then laid a clean white blouse waist in the hyacinth-scented drawer, thankful that George Garrity had offered her passage to Detroit by yacht. From there, the trip to Ann Arbor to enter the University of Michigan would be a fairly simple train ride of forty miles or less.

When she had unpacked a few belongings, she sat by the cabin window and watched as her island home receded in the distance, the white tower growing small and hazy in the early morning mist as the yacht made its way past North Manitou Island and Pyramid Point. She pulled her shawl about her shoulders against the damp morning air. The prospect of starting school in a strange new environment where the only person she knew was her teacher's longtime friend, Professor Overholt, was a little chilling. She had met him briefly at the University of Michigan exhibit at the Fair in 1893, and was thankful that her connection with Mrs. Garrity had brought his offer of room and board and tuition money in exchange for her assistance with research, and the domestic help she would give his wife at their home. Such an arrangement was the key to Charlotte's being able to afford a higher education.

Though adjusting to a whole new way of life was a daunting proposition, even more unnerving was the thought of being with Seth again. George had said he had left Seth in Detroit to supervise an important shipment of stoves that had to go out this week, but Charlotte wondered whether Seth had stayed behind because of his reluctance to see her again.

She would soon find out. Once in Detroit, Martha Garrity had invited her to stay overnight before going on to school, and had invited Seth to take dinner with them.

She reached inside the lacy stand-up collar on her cotton dress and pulled out the delicate gold chain and locket he had presented to her over four years ago. Opening the clasp, she removed the store photographs and reread the inscriptions, wondering whether they had any meaning.

She wondered, too, about Laura Ducharme. Maybe Seth had developed a serious romantic interest in her. Though he had sent Charlotte half a dozen letters in the last two years, they had made no mention of his feelings.

She tucked the locket back inside her collar, sat down at the writing desk where she had penned her remembrances of the Fair five years ago, and pulled out the bottom right hand drawer. Several small blank notebooks waited to be filled. She smiled to herself. The *Martha G.* hadn't changed much since she had last been aboard, and neither had her namesake.

Martha Garrity was still her same old crusty self, judging from the brief conversation Charlotte had just shared with her in the saloon. She still bore little tolerance for those in the world who were less wealthy, less educated, and didn't subscribe to her personal views on politics and religion, but one aspect of her was notably different. From the moment Charlotte had stepped aboard at South Manitou Island, Martha *had* treated her with respect, no doubt because of her acceptance at the University of Michigan.

Charlotte reached for her valise, taking out a handful of school children's papers, and began rereading the precious reminiscences of the past four years during which she had worked as an assistant to her former teacher.

> *My favorite memory was when you used to come outside with us in winter and play fox and geese . . .*
>
> *My favorite memory was of the Christmas program two years ago when you came dressed up as Mary . . .*
>
> *My favorite memory was the time you helped us make May baskets . . .*

The memories brought on a mild case of melancholy, now that the one-room school on her island home was a part of her past. In a way, she could hardly believe that the objective she had been striving for during the past four years was now reality, and that the beloved place would no longer be a part of her everyday life.

Two days aboard the *Martha G.* had proved pleasant, if uneventful, Charlotte thought, as she arranged her wicker chair on the afterdeck in the late afternoon sun. The expanse of Lake St. Clair lay behind her, and at the bow was the Detroit River. As they entered the narrows between the city and Belle Isle, the metropolitan shoreline bore some resemblance to the windy city she had visited five years earlier. An excursion steamer loading with passengers blew her whistle in preparation to leave her dock. Smoke-stacks belching soot contrasted with church belfries of glistening white. Red brick factories joined shoulders with brown frame warehouses, and "JEROME B. RICE SEED COMPANY" lettered in white on a dark façade came clearly into view.

As George brought his yacht around toward shore, she recognized the Michigan Stove Company sign above the vast expanse of a factory. Surely only minutes separated them from their landing. She touched the bodice of her dress, where the locket lay hidden beneath the green velvet fabric. Her heart fluttered. Would Seth welcome her, as she had him on their last meeting?

Seth kept watch for the *Martha G.* from the window beside the small oak desk in his spartan, smokestack-scented office overlooking the Detroit River. He was both longing for, and dreading the chance to see Charlie again. The feeling was no stranger. It had haunted him since the last time he had visited her on South Manitou. For the last two years, he had literally been held prisoner by it, and had chosen to avoid her except for the few missives he had penned.

The circumstances of their last parting had inflicted terrible, gut-wrenching pain. Being turned down by Charlie, with whom he had spent precious growing-up years, was like being rejected at his very own home! He wasn't sure he wanted to risk that kind of pain ever again. Not even for the girl of his dreams. At the same time, he couldn't deny his very real desire to see her again.

He reached for the oaken two-drawer file, pulled out a folder containing shipping papers, and shoved in the records of the order that had been sent to Chicago that morning. Despite his preoccupation with business for ten to twelve hours out of every working day, certain questions nagged at him.

Why did he love Charlie so much? Why did she have to be so much younger than he? Most of all, why did she feel compelled to continue her education? In all the hours he had spent trying to understand her, and himself, he had come to one conclusion. His troubles with her had begun the moment he stopped thinking of her as a sister. So many years had passed in the interim, he didn't think it was possible to revive that lighthearted, teasing rapport they had once shared. At eighteen, she was a woman, a fact he couldn't possibly hope to ignore.

And the fact that she would be only thirty-eight miles from Detroit while attending university held no solace for him. It had the opposite effect. She would be more accessible, and he more tempted to court her and convince her to let him make her his wife rather than pursue the B.A. degree for which she was about to enroll.

But such actions on his part would probably result in more pain. Besides, now that he had established a certain amount of financial security in George Garrity's employ, he was ready to take the next step. In fact, since Charlie had four years of schooling ahead of her, this might be a very good time to make the change he had been considering.

Further thoughts on the subject would have to wait. The *Martha G.* was headed for the pier, and he would be expected to welcome its arrival. He shoved the file folder back into the cabinet, tidied up his already neat desk, grabbed his suit jacket from the coat tree, and shrugged it on as he headed out the door.

The first moment Charlotte saw Seth on the dock helping to land the *Martha G.*, she wondered whether he were feeling well. She couldn't remember ever seeing him so sober-looking without good cause.

He appeared older, but then, a long time had passed since she had last seen him. His light brown hair was perfectly parted on the left, as usual, but it had started to thin a little.

He tied off a line, then looked up at her, flashing a wide smile showing the slight overlap in his front teeth, and Charlie knew he was truly pleased to see her.

The instant Seth laid eyes on Charlie, he knew his inner battle had begun again with a vengeance, and that it would be the toughest struggle yet. Though Charlie hadn't gained much in height beyond the five-feet-three inches he remembered of two years past, she had gained remarkably in attractiveness, with her caramel-colored hair loosely twisted into a knot atop her head, and her wide-set brown eyes gleaming in the afternoon sunshine. She could put Charles Dana Gibson's girls to shame, he thought!

He could hardly take his eyes off her long enough to help George drop the gangway. When he held her hand to assist her as she stepped onto the dock, he had to remind himself that while his heart shouted, *Never let go*, his head overruled with, *Enjoy the evening, then you must walk away*. He tried to think of some offhand remarks that would keep things on the lighter side.

"Welcome to Detroit, Charlie! I see the *Martha G.* managed to arrive all of a piece, despite your being on-board!"

Feeling more like the little girl he had teased en route to the Fair so many years ago, than the young lady to whom he had once proposed marriage, Charlotte impulsively hugged him and pecked his cheek, nearly dancing on his feet— which still seemed longer than necessary. How wonderful to feel his arms around her again, even if it were only for a brief, sibling-like embrace. She stood back, noticing how intriguing little lines at the corners of Seth's hazel eyes added maturity.

"Seth Trevelyn, I take no comfort in discovering your opinion of me hasn't changed since I was last aboard the *Martha G.* five years ago. I'll have you know I've behaved like a perfect lady since I left home. In fact, my cruise was disappointingly smooth," she informed him. "Not once did I go down to the engine room, though I was tempted to try to turn up the steam when Stokes wasn't looking!"

"You were in that much of a hurry to see me?" he teased, wishing it were true.

She scowled. "It's all your fault, of course. You write to me but three times a year, at most. You've stayed away from the island for two years running, and only visited once in the two years before that. I thought it likely George would have to reintroduce us!" She tried to be witty, but beneath it all, she wondered if he understood the pain she had suffered following their previous encounter.

"I'll never forget your face, Charlie, though I'll admit either my memory has taken a vacation, or you've grown prettier since my last trip to South Manitou." He offered his arm to escort her off the dock.

She slipped her hand inside his elbow and they followed George and his mother toward the stove works. "Flattery won't make up for your long absences, Seth Trevelyn. The least you could have done was answer my letters. You still owe me one!"

"And if I know you, you're not going to let me forget it."

"You know something? It seems like we're right back to old times. Together and . . . " Charlotte nearly said "arguing," but caught herself in time to say "teasing."

Seth laughed. "It's going to be an interesting night." *But not nearly long enough.*

Once inside George's office at the stove works, he insisted Seth show Charlotte his own office. George then made arrangements for her trunk to be sent to Ann Arbor, and for his driver to fetch them and take them to the house he shared with his mother where supper would be served.

Charlotte noted with interest that Seth's office differed very little from that of his boss, excepting that it was a trifle smaller with fewer windows looking out on the river.

When she had settled into the coach for the ride along Jefferson Avenue, the scene reminded her of Chicago when she had been driven from Mrs. Spencer's home to the pier where the *Martha G.* was tied up. Everyone seemed to be trying to get down the same streets at the same time. Coming from South Manitou Island, where two farm wagons constituted heavy traffic on the rutted dirt roads, it was quite unnerving!

The driver turned onto a street called Woodward which led away from the river. Charlotte was so intent on her conversation with Seth, catching up on two years' worth of news, that the next thing she knew, the coach had entered a driveway beside a large pink brick home.

It was an imposing structure with a two-story wrap-around veranda, a tower and witch's cap ascending beyond the upper left corner of the third floor, three huge chimneys rising amidst the gables, and a red tile roof. A generous yard surrounded the home, and a two-story carriage house stood at the end of the long driveway.

The maid greeted them at the *porte cochère* and, while George made certain his carriage and team were properly tended by hired hands, the domestic welcomed them into the foyer. Charlotte found the interior of the home equally impressive, starting with the magnificent walnut flying staircase which wound upward through three stories.

"The stairway took a year and a half to build," Martha bragged. "Only a handful of people have ever commissioned one as grand."

When the elderly woman had moved on, Charlotte couldn't help exchanging grins with Seth.

He leaned down, whispering in her ear. "I've heard her say that at least a dozen times in the last five years."

In the spacious parlor, Charlotte admired the large hand-cast white plaster medallion that dominated the center of the rose-colored ceiling. From it hung a graceful chandelier which enhanced the soft light filtering through the sheers on the huge bay windows. In the bay was a grand piano, and on its shiny lacquer lid, several small photographic portraits in ovals, squares, and circles of antique brass.

On the walls were paintings that reminded Charlotte of the Renaissance art she had seen at the World's Columbian Exposition. Their wide frames had been hand-carved and gold-leafed. The cut glass bowl of potpourri on a cherry table filled the room with a delicious gardenia scent, while the coverings on an Empire style divan, matching love seat, and a pair of Queen Anne chairs on either side of the fireplace offered an Oriental flavor.

"This furniture is upholstered with cut-up Persian rugs," Martha explained proudly. "The Stuarts—candy tycoons of New York City—came up with the idea. Isn't it a marvelous way to make use of old carpets?" Before Charlotte could offer an opinion, Martha gestured toward the love seat. "Why don't you two young people rest your feet, and I'll see if Pearl is nearly ready with dinner."

In his mother's absence, George sat down to play the piano. Charlotte was surprised at his talent, but knew she shouldn't have been. After all, he had changed so much over the past five years that she never knew quite what to expect from one time to the next. She sometimes wondered how her teacher could remain unaffected by his attentions.

Within minutes, Martha announced that dinner would be served. When Seth seated Charlotte at the black walnut dining table, she realized nothing about the house was of ordinary size. Expansive walnut sideboards and shelves ran the length of the spacious room. In its center, a chandelier with thousands of crystals hung from the ceiling. At the end of the room, a windowed alcove provided the perfect showcase for the silver Regency tea service, glistening atop a lace-covered table.

At the end of the sumptuous meal, which had consisted of five courses from potato and leek soup to cherry-topped cheesecake, George suggested that Seth take his cabriolet and show Charlotte the neighborhood.

He drove along Woodward Avenue past half a dozen homes every bit as large as the Garritys', while Charlotte searched her memory for all the news she could think of from home, the most important of which seemed to be Aurora's upcoming wedding to Harrison Stone, planned for Thanksgiving Day. An hour passed quickly, and too soon the flaming red ball had sunk low, painting the sky with bold orange streaks. On their return to the pink brick mansion, Charlotte noticed the enchanting gazebo in the back yard.

"Let's sit outdoors for a while," she suggested as Seth helped her down from the buggy. In the moist evening air hung the scent of the roses that rambled over trellis and fence, and the strains of the "Merry Widow Waltz" from the piano in the parlor.

She took a seat on the gazebo bench while Seth, his back to her, leaned against one of the posts, gazing into the distance. She wondered what must be going through his mind. Moments later, he sat down beside her.

"Charlie, seeing you again and hearing about the island makes me realize how much I've missed out on these last five years. It's just not the same living down here, working for George." For the first time since her arrival, his tone had changed from teasing to reverent.

Though she wanted to ask why he had allowed such long periods to lapse between visits, her curiosity was overshadowed by her relief in knowing that despite their last encounter, he obviously still cared a great deal for her.

He cast a glance in the direction of the house, then continued thoughtfully. "Can you keep a secret?"

She nodded.

"I've promised myself that someday I'm going to get back to the island and be my own boss. Please don't mention this to anyone. I couldn't bear for George to think

I plan to betray him after all he's taught me. I'll stay in Detroit a while longer, but city life's not for me. Maybe by the time you've finished your degree, I'll be an independent businessman."

He seemed to be implying he would wait for her. Was it possible he was no longer interested in Laura? Her name hadn't come up once, and she wasn't about to ask.

"I'm glad you said something. I had thought maybe you didn't like me or the island anymore."

Seth threw his head back and laughed. Still chuckling, he picked up her hand, squeezed it firmly three times, then three more in a long-short-long pattern. She repeated the code back to him, then he let go, making a point to return her hand to her lap.

Leaning his elbows on his knees, he looked down, deep in thought. Charlotte wondered what must be going through his mind. Unconsciously, her hand moved to the bodice of her dress, and she was reminded of the locket. She pulled it out, arranging it against the green velvet fabric.

After a few silent moments, Seth raised his greenish-brown eyes to hers, as if looking into her soul. Quietly, he stated, "There's never been anyone for me but you, Charlie."

How badly she wanted to throw her arms about him and kiss him! But she restrained herself. "Oh, Seth, I feel the same about you! I've missed you so very much since you moved away. At least now, we'll be less than forty miles apart. Mrs. Garrity tells me the trains run constantly between Ann Arbor and Detroit, and they're very efficient. We can see each other almost anytime we want!"

A muscle in Seth's cheek twitched. "No. We can't."

His words held a quiet resolve.

She opened her mouth to protest, but he continued.

"You need time to adjust to your new life at school. Studying will occupy most of your hours, and new friends, the remainder of them. You don't need me getting in the way."

"Seth, how can you say such a thing?" she quickly challenged. "You won't be in the way!"

"Charlie, will you do one thing for me?" he asked solemnly.

"Of course, Seth."

"Give yourself from now until Thanksgiving to settle in at the university. When the holiday comes, I promise we'll share a turkey dinner together."

She regretted her earlier compliance, but felt helpless to renege. "You're being awfully pushy about this," she complained, "but I can see you've made up your mind."

"Good. I'm glad we understand each other." His hazel eyes lowered to the locket. He seemed to be noticing it for the first time. "Isn't that—"

"Yes, it's the locket you gave me." She stroked it fondly. "Do you remember the message you had inscribed in it?"

"Of course I do," he said, taking offense at the question. "I feel the same—no, stronger—today about you than I did when I had it engraved."

"Then will you explain something to me?" she asked sweetly, sensing her advantage. "If you care about me the way you say you do, why do you stay away so long?"

He sighed. "Someday, I'll explain it to you, but not now. It's time I take my leave." He stood and held his hand out, then pulled her up off the bench. He continued to hold her hand as he walked her to the door beneath the *porte cochère*. Before she could even organize the words for a proper good-bye, he bent and kissed her on the cheek, then backed away. "Good luck with school, Charlie. I'll be thinking of you. See you in a couple of months."

CHAPTER 19

November 1898

Four blocks upriver from the stove works, Seth stood on the deck of the gleaming white steamer with its owner, wrapped his scarf tighter about his neck against the icy, wind-whipped snowflakes, and waved both arms above his head.

"Nat! Over here!"

His older brother lifted his gloved hand and quickened his pace, stepping aboard the vessel moments later.

Seth made introductions. "Nat, this is Captain Elliott. Captain, my brother, Nat."

The short, woolen-clad man of about sixty offered his hand. "Pleased to meet ya. Y'r brother tells me the two of ya are plannin' to run a route up north next season."

Nat pumped Elliott's hand twice. "Yes, sir. If we can find the right vessel, that is."

"My *Nellie* is a fine steamer. Real steady in rough weather. Tight bilge, too. Don't need to worry none about takin' on water. And she's got plenty of capacity for a seventy-five footer. You'll earn back your investment in no time!" He gestured toward the stairs going below. "C'mon. I'll show ya around."

Seth and his brother followed the spry gentleman down the short flight of steps to the boiler which was banked with fire. Elliott had already shown Seth proof of registration and government inspection last spring, but a season had passed in the interim, and without proper upkeep, mechanical problems could develop. From his years crewing for Stokes, Seth knew what to look for, and began a systematic check of the Thomas McGregor Works boiler from ash pan to smoke stack, looking for any sign of weakness in braces. He took note, too, of the instruments—the pop safety valve, check and blow-off valves, steam and water gauges, compression gauges, cocks and whistle. He would need to observe them while underway in order to determine whether they were functional.

After a thorough inspection of the firing tools, he turned to Captain Elliott. "If you'll take Nat up above, he can look over the pilothouse, controls, and deck while I check the interior of the hull."

"Will do, but I can guarantee you'll find everything in order, Mr. Trevelyn, just as your brother will up top." He took a lantern from a hook and lit it, handing it to Seth. "This'll help convince you. When you're done, we can cast off and take her downriver a piece so's the two of ya can see how she handles."

Seth took the lantern and the ice pick he'd kept hidden in his coat pocket, and crawled into the narrow compartment at the bow between the hull and deck, eager to learn whether the shiny coat of exterior paint was just a cover-up, or the hull was really as solid as Captain Elliott would have him believe. In cramped quarters, he began a systematic check of planks and ribs, paying close attention for any sign of loose, missing, or corroded fastenings, sticking his ice pick into the wood at the waterline to check for wood rot. As he inspected behind bulkheads, inside bilges, and every other tight spot, he wondered what Nat was finding topside. If there were no moisture problems around deck fittings and hatches, and if the anchor, chain, rails and deck braces were solid, he was certain his brother would be eager to try his hand at the wheel under steam.

The thought of actually making an offer on the vessel was somewhat daunting. The captain was asking a fair price, and would probably even come down on it at this time of year. Seth felt confident that he and his brother could work a deal, with some bank financing, but the thought of going so heavily into debt was enough to make his knees weak.

Even so, in the past several weeks, he had come to the conclusion it would be better for the two of them to strike out on their own now, than to wait. With Charlie in Ann Arbor, he'd nearly had to handcuff himself to his desk at the stove works in order to keep from getting on the train and going over there to see her. If this deal worked out, he was wondering how he'd be able to tell her he would be sailing for South Manitou and couldn't keep his promise to dine with her on Thanksgiving. He'd have to pay a call and tell her in person. And if he did that, he wouldn't want to leave her.

He put concerns over Charlie aside for the moment and inched his way toward the stern. The ice pick sunk a little too easily into one of the planks. He checked thoroughly for further indications of wood rot on each side of the transom. It seemed to be limited to four planks near the waterline. They could be replaced early next spring at the yard in Frankfort, a lever to help bring Elliott down on his asking price.

He crawled backward, working his way out of the tight places, and headed up to the deck. Of the three steamers he and Nat had looked at this month, the hull on *Nellie* was the most solid. If Nat was finding her in good condition topside, she would be the best buy for the money.

A brown folio beneath his arm, Seth paused outside George Garrity's office and took a deep breath. Since he and Nat had closed the deal with Captain Elliott at the bank yesterday afternoon, he had been anticipating this moment with dread. In fact, he had put it off all morning, but now that lunch was over and everyone had settled back into their work, it was time to break the news.

Through the window in the oak door, he could see George bent over his untidy desk, shuffling paperwork with a scowl. His boss paused to scratch the stubble on his chin, a resurgence of the beard he had been growing back since his return from South Manitou Island in the end of September. He'd been a bear since that trip. Seth suspected it had something to do with Helen, but George had been avoiding the subject.

Nevertheless, the subject of the *Manitou Lady*, the new name Nat and Seth had chosen for their vessel, couldn't be avoided. He turned the brass doorknob and stepped up to George's desk with a confidence he didn't feel.

George barely looked up. "What is it, Seth? I'm busy," he said sourly. When Seth hesitated a moment, George glared up at him. "Speak up, son. I haven't got all day!"

Seth whipped out a letter and offered it to George. "I've come to tender my resignation as of Friday, next."

George's face colored. He glanced momentarily at the

document without touching it, then slowly rose, leaning across his desk into Seth's face, staring wide-eyed. "You *what?*" he barked.

Seth lowered the piece of paper with a shaky hand and let it drop on top of several others in the center of the oak desk. Summoning up his confidence, he repeated forcefully, "I've come to tender my resignation, sir." Without breaking eye contact, he opened his brown folio and removed the architectural renderings of *Nellie* that Captain Elliott had given him. "My brother, Nat, and I are going into the shipping business up north next season. We've bought a small steamer and will be taking her up there next Saturday."

George batted aside the blueprints, sending them to the floor. "That's a fine thanks I get for all I've done for you! Five years of teaching and training." George stalked angrily around his desk, backing Seth toward the door. "I was planning on making you a partner in the business next year. You would have shared the profits. Do you know what kind of money you could have made?"

Seth's back against the wall, he dared not answer.

George swung open his door. "Now get out of here! And clear out that desk of yours. You're finished!"

Seth ducked out the door just in time to keep from being hit when it slammed shut. He expected to hear the tinkling of broken glass hitting the floor, but an eerie silence ensued.

Numb, he went mechanically through the motions of finding a small crate in which to pack his personal effects. The numbness changed to controlled panic as he filled the box with the extra shirt, collars, and cuffs he had kept on hand for times when important men called at the stove works, and he couldn't get home to change before taking them out to dinner.

Anger crept over him as he collected the pens, nibs, cuff links, and a watch fob his former boss had given him as gifts over the years. How could George be so cruel, after having treated him like a favorite nephew for more than five years?

Seth had been counting on his last paycheck from the stove works to help pay for winter repairs on the boat. Now he would have to find some other way to come up with the funds.

He began checking the paperwork pending in the basket on his desk, attaching notes so whoever stepped into his job would know how to proceed.

Two hours after George had thrown him out of his office, Seth picked up his crate and put it under his arm. Hand on his doorknob, he was taking one last look around his office when his former boss barged in, colliding with him and nearly knocking the wooden box to the floor.

Together, they managed to steady it, then George took it away from Seth. "Where do you think you're going?" George demanded, setting the box in the corner by the coat tree. "Sit down. I want to talk with you."

Seth sat behind his desk, and George pulled up the straight chair opposite him. Pulling a sheaf of papers from his inside pocket, he slapped them down on Seth's empty ink blotter, extracting a narrow strip of paper from the folded stack.

"If you're going into business, you could make good use of this, I presume." He placed a check for five hundred dollars in front of Seth. "And I won't have you leaving here without your last paycheck and some severance money." Another check appeared in the amount of one month's salary.

Opening the sheaf of folded papers, he handed Seth the blueprints of the *Nellie*. "I sure hope this bathtub floats. I wouldn't want you sinking before you deliver your first load."

"She floats, sir! Guaranteed! And her engine and boiler are in fine condition, too," Seth offered enthusiastically.

George spread a document atop the architectural drawings. "Good! Because these stoves have *got* to get to my customers up north before winter sets in. See to it you're at the dock by seven sharp next Saturday morning to load them up!"

He shoved back his chair and started to leave. Seth was still staring in disbelief at the checks and bill of lading when George paused, his hand on the doorknob, and turned to him. "Don't just sit there, son! You're an independent businessman now!" He shook a finger at him. "You've got to hustle! Now get out of here!"

Seth wasted no time setting off toward the bank. His next destination was the train station, and by late afternoon, he was en route to Ann Arbor to see Charlie. He sat watching the bare trees, windblown leaves, and harvested fields roll by—dreary scenery on an overcast afternoon. The rapid *clack, clack, clack,* of the rails lulled him into a world apart, a world not defined by iron track and stuffy passenger cars, but by wind, water, and a wooden hull. He and Nat were aboard the *Manitou Lady* making good time toward the Straits of Mackinac. Charlie was there, too.

Suddenly, the train whistle blew, startling him from his

reverie. He unbuttoned his coat, and from his pocket, pulled the only letter Charlie had sent him and reread it.

October 16, 1898
Dear Seth,

I am not accustomed to so many people in one place. The University Hall seems crowded. When classes are in session, it holds more people than actually live on our little island in the lake!

I am only one of nearly six hundred women students in the literary department! I received an A on my first assignment. My good study habits have paid off, though I have so much work to do helping Prof. Overholt organize his research, and Mrs. Overholt preparing the evening meal each day that I sometimes stay up well past midnight reading my literature assignments.

I'm already looking forward to Thanksgiving with you and the Garritys at their place. It will be nice to have a little time with you.

I will see you in November.
Fondly,
Charlotte

Seth folded the letter and slipped it back into his pocket. He could tell Charlotte would take it hard when she learned he would be on South Manitou Island by Thanksgiving, especially with Aurora getting married that day.

He stared out the window at the landscape again, eager to be on the lake with Nat in a few more days. Even though he and his brother had been planning their move for the past four weeks, it still seemed impossible to believe that they had actually struck out on their own. He made a mental list of all he must accomplish before they left Detroit with George Garrity's stoves.

Before he was ready, it seemed, the train arrived at the Ann Arbor depot. He asked directions to the street where Charlie was living with the Overholts and set off on foot to find her. A quarter of an hour later, he was on the front walk of the two-story Federal style brick home. By his timepiece, it was a few minutes before six. She would probably be there helping to prepare the evening meal. He stepped purposefully up to the white door and cranked the brass bell.

The door opened slowly at first, then suddenly, Charlie was standing there, a long white apron over her waist and skirt. Though little shadows beneath her brown eyes hinted at fatigue, a smile quickly lit them with sparkling chips of topaz.

"Seth! What a wonderful surprise! Come in!" She pulled him by the arm into the front hallway. The cozy warmth of a fireplace fire welcomed him, as well as the aroma of fresh baked goods.

Seth took off his cap and turned it in his hands, trying to forget how badly he wanted to wrap his arms about her small waist and bury his face in her wavy hair. Instead, he offered a smile. "Hello, Charlie. It's good to see you."

She took his cap and hung it on the coat tree. "Professor Overholt and his wife and daughter have gone to his sister's for supper. I'm fixing soup for myself. Take off your coat and make yourself at home in the parlor." She indicated the front room to his left. "I'll add some beef and vegetables to the pot, and set another place." She hurried off.

Seth was drawn to the fireplace. The fire was burning low. He threw in two sticks. They crackled and popped while he warmed his hands. He sat on the end of a green velvet Empire sofa, too edgy to lean against its gracefully curved arm, and pulled out some small sketches he had made of the *Manitou Lady*. When he heard Charlie coming, he rose, stuffing them back into his pocket.

Charlie came to sit beside him, her face still alight with pleasure as it had been when she'd first opened the door. "I can't tell you how glad I am that you're here! I hadn't counted on seeing you until I came to Detroit. What brings you this way?"

Unable to smile, Seth reached for Charlie's hand. It was red and chapped, evidently from the work she had been doing for Mrs. Overholt. He folded it securely within his own, wishing he could take her away from this place, longing for more time with her than just this one evening. He cleared his throat and forced himself to speak. "I have some important news. I know I promised we'd have Thanksgiving dinner together, but there's been a change in plans." He paused for the objections he was sure would come, but Charlie sat quietly, waiting for him to continue. "Do you remember my telling you about wanting to go back to the island and be an independent businessman someday?"

"Yes. Go on," she urged.

Reluctantly, he let go of her hand to take out the sketches of the *Manitou Lady*. "Nat and I bought a boat yesterday. We're going into the shipping business. On Saturday, we're heading north with our first load. We'll be spending Thanksgiving on the island, then we're taking the boat to Frankfort to leave her for the winter."

Charlie's eyes opened wide, filling with moisture as she stared at his drawings of the boat.

The sight of her tears caused a wrench to twist in Seth's stomach. Quickly, he tried to explain. "Please don't be sad, Charlie. We'll have this evening together before I go. Then I have to move far away from you." He lifted her tear-stained face, looking into her misty brown eyes. "You see, I just couldn't stand it anymore, knowing we weren't even fifty miles apart. Ever since you came down from South Manitou, I've wanted nothing more than to be with you. After a while, I realized it's time for me to get back to South Manitou. If I can't be with the girl I love, then I'm going to the place I love to wait until you've finished your schooling." He wiped away her tear with his thumb.

Without a word, Charlie gave back the sketches of the *Manitou Lady* and took him by the hand, offering him a strange half-smile as she pulled him up from the sofa and led him through the center hallway toward the back of the house.

"Where are we going?"

"You'll see."

He followed her through the kitchen. She opened the back door. A cold blast of air hit him as he stepped onto a dark porch. From the kitchen, a shaft of light spilled onto Charlie's trunk. Quickly, she unfastened the straps and flung open the lid. It was heaped to the top with her personal effects.

She looked up at him, the pale light revealing a beaming smile. "You'd better make room aboard the *Manitou Lady* for one more passenger and trunk, because I'm going to South Manitou with you!"

Though Seth had heard every word, he was certain he

had misunderstood. "You're *what*?"

Shivering, she closed the lid. "I'm quitting school!" she said triumphantly. "I've thought about it for weeks. Yesterday, I made up my mind I'd get home in time for Thanksgiving, for Aurora's wedding. I was planning to come to Detroit tomorrow to tell you."

Seth still couldn't make sense of it. "But . . . what about the university? Your degree?"

Shaking from the cold, she rubbed her arms briskly. "It's not important. Not compared to happiness. The most important thing I've learned is that book learning isn't everything! But being a good daughter, a good sister, a good . . . friend . . .*is*." She looked up at him with eyes shining. "Besides, I've missed you so much since September, I couldn't concentrate on my studies anyway!"

At last, the meaning of what she was telling him began to sink in. He wrapped his arms about her, crushing her to him, pressing her face to his chest. "Oh, Charlie!" His voice was husky with emotion. "I love you so much, I didn't know how I was going to be able to leave you again!"

Seth's reaction sent Charlotte's spirits soaring. She worked her arms around him, squeezing as tightly as she could, wishing the embrace would never end. "I've been so lonely without you, Seth!"

For several moments, Seth held her snugly, then slowly released her. He took her face in his hands. Even in the wan light, he could see that her eyes were sparkling with tears of joy.

Then Seth quietly posed the question that had caused such agony on an earlier occasion.

"Charlie—" he spoke her name softly. "I'm going to

ask you again—will you marry me?"

Charlotte pushed herself out of his arms just enough to be able to see him clearly. Then she cocked her head and furrowed her brow in mock dismay. "Seth Trevelyn, if you think I'm going to turn you down *this* time—The answer is Yes, Yes, Yes!"

Her last words were muffled against his shoulder as he scooped her up again and lifted her off her feet, holding her so tightly she could hardly breathe!

CHAPTER 20

Snow fell lightly from the dusky sky as the *Manitou Lady* came into the curved harbor past the light atop the South Manitou tower. Bundled from head to toe against the wintry weather, Charlotte watched the approach from the pilothouse with Nat. The chill she had been feeling in the air since leaving Detroit four days earlier dissipated in the welcome sent by the steady white beam, and the knowledge that she would soon be warming herself by the fire in the keeper's quarters, at home once more on her beloved island.

So much had happened since she had left Ann Arbor only two weeks earlier. Seth had brought her to stay in his apartment while he and Nat lived on the boat at dockside, fitting her out for the run north. Together, the three of them had managed to deliver all but one of the stoves George had loaded onto the *Manitou Lady*. Charlotte had helped drop the cork fenders over the side each time they came into a dock, and had assisted in notifying merchants at Cheboygan, Mackinaw City, Petoskey, and Charlevoix that their merchandise had arrived at the pier. She had kept the shipping papers up to date and in an orderly file, as well. It pleased her, knowing she had been of some help to the Trevelyn brothers' upstart shipping concern on their first voyage.

The last stove—would soon be delivered at South Manitou—a fancy model destined for George's sister-in-law. Nat and Seth would take it to her as soon as they came into port, and install it later in the week, after tomorrow's wedding and Thanksgiving Day feast, and their return from Frankfort where they would be taking the *Manitou Lady* on Friday.

Charlotte had given much consideration to what she would say to Mrs. Garrity. The thought of seeing her again was a bit unnerving. She wanted desperately not to disappoint the woman she idolized, the individual who had been the greatest influence on her in the past five years. Time and again, Mrs. Garrity had predicted that Charlotte would one day graduate from the University of Michigan with her Bachelor of Arts degree in literature. Charlotte prayed her mentor would understand the reasons for her change in plans.

After a quick trip to the keeper's quarters where Charlotte's mother had served up roast beef sandwiches, Seth and Nat had hitched up the wagon, and Charlotte had returned with them to the dock to load up and deliver the teacher's new stove. She felt like the meat in the sandwich, perched between the brothers on the seat of the wagon carrying the stove over the rutted road to Mrs. Garrity's.

Wind off the lake whipped at her scarf, biting at the exposed areas of her face. Seth's arm tightened about her, shielding her from the blustery weather that was rapidly moving up from the southwest.

Within minutes, they were in sight of the cottage. Nat reined in, bringing the wagon to a halt alongside the house, where lantern light leaked past the sheer curtains at Helen's small front windows. Seth helped Charlotte down, lifting her easily from the high wagon seat, and while he and his brother set about removing the crated stove from the wagon bed, she rapped on her teacher's front door.

Moments later, Helen opened it. Her face lit up with surprise. "Charlie Richards! Of all people, I never expected . . . " Her attention was diverted to Seth and Nat. "What—?"

"We've brought you a gift!" Charlotte hastily explained.

Helen stepped outside, pulling her shawl closer about her. "Sakes alive! I can't imagine . . . "

When the crate was positioned temporarily beside the house, Seth explained. "Compliments of Mr. George Garrity, one Michigan Stove Works cookstove, six-hole, with high and low closets and reservoir. Comes complete with installation, to be done at your convenience later this week!"

Helen stepped up to the huge wooden box. In the soft light cast through the window, Charlotte glimpsed the wide-eyed look on her face. "Oh, my! I hardly know what to say, except—thank you! Now, won't you all come inside? The least I can do is offer you some hot tea for your efforts on this wintry eve."

Nat tipped his cap. "Thanks for your kindness, ma'am, but I'd best get on home to my wife. It's been better than two months since I've seen her." He laid a hand on his brother's shoulder. "It's but a short ways to Meta's folks.

I'll leave the wagon for you and Charlie. See you both tomorrow." Swiftly, he took off, leaving a trail in the light dusting of snow that had begun to cover the narrow road.

"Seth, Charlie, surely the two of you can come inside and warm yourselves a spell before going home? I have a fresh pot of tea already made."

Charlotte felt Seth's nudge at the small of her back, giving her courage to accept. "We'd love to—for just a little while. Our folks are anxious to have us home."

Helen insisted Charlotte and Seth sit on the love seat by the parlor stove while she went to the kitchen to pour tea. She returned to sit across from them in her white wicker chair, placing the silver tray bearing flowered china cups filled with steaming Earl Gray tea and a plate of tiny butter cookies on the table between.

Helen sipped from her cup, then held it in her lap. "I still can't get over the fact that you're here!" she said in a voice that was taut with some unnamed tension. "I suppose you'll be returning to school right after your sister's wedding," she said to Charlotte. To Seth, she said, "And I can't imagine George allowing you more than a day or two's leave at this time of year."

Charlotte glanced at Seth, waiting for him to answer, but his only response was a nod of encouragement, and slight nudge from his elbow. Charlotte's feelings seesawed between the elation of being betrothed and the fear of disappointing the woman who held such a special place in her heart. "Seth and I have some news," she said brightly, trying to hide her apprehension. "We've decided to get married!"

Helen's brows lifted and a courteous smile followed. "Then congratulations and best wishes are in order! When is the happy event?"

Again, Charlotte glanced at Seth, and again he deferred. "We haven't actually set a date," she explained. "We thought it best to decide after Aurora's wedding. Perhaps in the spring."

Helen sipped her tea, then passed the plate of cookies that had thus far been neglected, still finding no takers. "A spring wedding will be lovely," she concluded stiffly, returning the full plate to the tray. "By then, you'll have nearly finished your first year at the university."

Charlotte heard the disappointment in her teacher's voice, saw it in her ill attempt to smile, and looked down. She fussed with the fold of her skirt. Seth covered her hand with his, giving her the confidence to look directly into her teacher's clear blue eyes and finish her explanation. "I'm not going back to school, Mrs. Garrity," she solemnly admitted. "I missed the island more than words can say—you, and the school children—and I missed Seth." She rushed on. "I figured if I couldn't be with Seth, at least I could come back to South Manitou, and maybe you'd let me help you again like I used to. I had my trunk all packed when Seth came to Ann Arbor to tell me he had resigned from the stove works to go into the shipping business with a boat he and Nat had bought. That's when we decided to get married."

Furrows appeared above Helen's brow. She seemed to be struggling to take in all that had been said. "Left school . . . resigned from the stove works . . . "

Charlotte chewed the inside of her lip. She hated thinking she had let her teacher down. Just as she felt her stomach knot, Seth squeezed her hand in their special code—three long squeezes, then a long-short-long—reminding her that everything would be okay.

Charlotte spoke again, trying to fill the gap in the conversation. "The Overholts send their regards. They say they always have a place for you if you should ever decide to leave the island."

"How kind of them," said Helen distractedly. She turned to Seth. "Poor George. He'll be lost without you. How is he, anyway?"

Seth offered the teacher his slow, lopsided smile, wondering how much of the truth to tell. "He's . . . George. Bossy, demanding . . . to be perfectly honest, he hasn't been quite himself since his last trip up here in September. It's almost as if—"

"As if what, Seth?" Helen asked quickly.

Seth took his time answering. "I don't like to speak unkindly of anyone, understand, but something must be bothering him. He's been more ornery than usual these past two months, and I'm not the only one who's noticed."

Helen had been listening intently. "I'm sorry to hear that, Seth. I've not heard a word from him since he came calling." She paused, evidently pondering the conundrum. Then, as if a new thought took over, a smile tipped the corners of her mouth, spread into a wide grin, and eventually encompassed her entire face, setting her eyes alight with pleasure. Turning to Charlotte, she exclaimed, "How wonderful that you're back to stay! The children and I will be more than happy to have you with us at school! To tell the truth, it just hasn't been the same since you left!" For the next several minutes, she told of some of the students and their progress since September. When the teacups were empty, she offered a refill.

Charlotte set her empty cup on the tray. "We really

should be going before it gets any later. Tomorrow's a big day, with nearly everyone on the island expected at the keeper's quarters at six for Aurora's wedding reception. You'll be there, won't you?"

"Of course. I wouldn't miss it."

At the door, Seth helped Charlotte into her coat, reminding the teacher of his promise to install the new stove. "Nat and I will be back to do the job after we've taken our boat to Frankfort. We're heading there Friday to leave her for the winter."

"You come when you can. I'm sure my present cookstove will hold out until then."

"Good night, Mrs. Garrity." Charlotte hugged her teacher's shoulders.

Helen returned the affection. "Good night Charlie. Good night, Seth. And thank you, both!"

Leaving Mr. Trevelyn and Seth to stand vigil, Charlotte hurried down the drafty tower stairs from the cold watch room and through the passage to the keeper's quarters, where her mother's roast turkey and freshly baked butterscotch rolls had already permeated the air with delicious aromas. She could hear the gusty wind rattling the office windows as she hung her coat in the back hallway. Climbing the stairs to her bedroom where Aurora was putting on her wedding gown, she dreaded being the bearer of bad news.

When she opened the door, her sister was looking through a clear patch she had scraped in the frosted window, a warm robe pulled about her corset and petticoats. Though her wedding was scheduled to begin in the parlor in forty-five minutes, the beaded satin dress she had labored over for the past six months still hung on the outside of the closet door.

"Any sign of Harrison's boat yet?" Aurora asked anxiously.

"No sign," Charlotte said with concern.

Aurora paced across the floor, chewing on her knuckle. "He said he and the preacher were going to leave Glen Arbor at daybreak. It seemed like good sailing weather until the wind picked up. But if he's not in sight, I suppose there's no hope of his getting here by four o'clock, is there?"

Charlotte crossed to the window that looked out on the passage and tower and a small piece of the harbor to the north. Snow was falling. A few minutes ago, she had been able to see well up the passage. Now, millions of white flakes were swirling in the wind as if never to touch down, making it impossible to see more than a few hundred yards from shore. "I'm afraid you're right. What's more, the waves are getting higher."

Aurora sighed. "Poor Mother. We had so carefully planned the hour of the private ceremony and dinner so we would be ready for our neighbors to come for the cake and punch reception at six." She crossed to the closet and took down her dress. "Harrison will be here soon," she said with new confidence, "now help me into my dress. I want to be ready so the ceremony can begin without delay once he arrives."

She laid the ensemble across her bed and was unpinning its flowing train from the hanger when a knock sounded on the door. Julia Richards let herself in. "Charlotte, Seth and his father would like a word with you downstairs. You'll find them in the office. I'll help Aurora."

Charlotte paused in the hallway outside the front sitting room. She couldn't help the melancholy feeling that came over her at the sight of the wedding cake her mother had painstakingly decorated with pastry flowers, and the garlands of silk myrtle and roses that Aurora had wired and draped from the table. At least they would keep if the ceremony were postponed, but she hoped that wouldn't be necessary.

She hurried down the hallway toward the office. From the basement kitchen, Bridget's and Mrs. Trevelyn's voices could be heard warning Dorin and Eli to stay away from the turkey and fixings until dinner time.

When she entered the office, Mr. Trevelyn and Seth were standing by the desk, talking quietly. Seth took her hand in his as she came beside him. "The direction the wind's blowing now, Harrison and the preacher will never make it, coming from the mainland. Dad thinks Nat and I should go find him and tow him in with the *Manitou Lady* if there's to be any wedding at all tonight."

"Poor Aurora," Charlotte sighed.

"Your mother's telling her now," Mr. Trevelyn said. "She said the turkey was done ahead of schedule, and she's put Mrs. Trevelyn and Bridget to work packing dinner buckets to send with the boys. With real good luck, we might have the groom and preacher here in another four hours. It will take at least a couple of hours for the boys to take on wood and stoke the boiler." He checked his timepiece. "I'll take one last look for a sail, but I don't expect I'll be able to see much."

When his father had gone, Seth closed the door and wrapped his arms loosely about Charlotte. "I hate to leave you, Charlie."

She put her arms about his neck. "I hate for you to go out in such nasty weather. Maybe I should go with you."

Seth smiled his lopsided grin and pressed her head against his chest, pulling her closer. "No, Charlie. While Nat and I are out in the cold, I want to know the girl I love is here, safe and warm, waiting for me."

She would have been content to remain in the shelter of Seth's arms indefinitely, but with the next gust of breeze to rattle the office windows, he loosed his embrace. "I'd better go now, before I find it impossible to walk away from you." Gently, he took her face in his hands and bent to press his lips against hers.

The brief kiss set Charlotte's pulse aflutter. She reached out for him, but he slipped away, leaving her with knees too shaky to follow.

CHAPTER 21

Charlotte stood on the tower balcony waving both hands wildly above her head. On the deck of the *Manitou Lady*, Seth waved back as the boat took him toward Glen Arbor.

She stayed on the cold balcony until he was out of sight, then stepped inside and closed the door. A strange feeling came over her, a dark foreboding. She recalled a time in her childhood when she had climbed to the balcony to watch a boat bound for Glen Arbor, only she had remained hidden inside the tower. And the man who had stood on the deck of the boat waving to her had never returned.

Her heart caught in her throat. For one excruciating moment, she recalled the pain of losing her father, pain that only lessened over time as Seth helped her to overcome her heartache. But if something happened to Seth now—

She couldn't bear to think of it. Down the spiral stairs she flew, as if trying to outrun the haunting ghost of a memory from her past.

The bedroom was cold and dark when Charlotte entered with the dinner tray for Aurora. In the dim light that seeped through the window from the lighthouse tower,

Charlotte could make out her eldest sister seated in a rocking chair by the frosty window, blotting her face with a handkerchief. Her wedding gown still lay across her bed. No one had blamed her for wanting to be alone rather than taking her meal with the rest of the family. Charlotte had barely tasted the food she had just eaten, and she certainly had not been hungry, but she had gone through the exercise in an effort to distract herself from her worry about Seth.

The plan had failed dismally. The southwest wind hit the dining room windows forcefully throughout dinner. Conversation had been so sparse that the rattling glass had predominated. By the time dessert was served, the pinging of freezing rain had stolen everyone's attention, making Charlotte even more anxious than before.

Now, guests were arriving for the wedding reception. The rain had turned to white flakes once again. Still there was no sign of the groom and preacher, nor any indication that the snowfall, now heavy enough to obscure the steady white light of the tower from any great distance, would soon let up.

Charlotte shoved those dismal thoughts aside and crossed the room, coming to stand beside Aurora. Her sister's puffy eyes glistened with dampness. Charlotte spoke softly. "I've brought you some dinner—turkey, dressing, gravy, squash, and a piece of Mama's pumpkin pie."

Several silent moments lapsed, filled only by the soft scraping sound as Aurora cleared frost from the glass with a letter opener. Her attention remained on the window as she spoke. "I'm not hungry."

Charlotte set the tray on the night stand and pulled her woolen shawl more tightly about her shoulders. "I'll leave it in case you want something later." She had turned to go when her sister started crying again. Charlotte knelt beside Aurora, putting her arm about her shoulders. "Everything will be all right. You'll see." Even to her own ears, the words sounded hollow. In truth, she was scared silly that in an effort to save Harrison and Preacher Mulder, both Seth and Nat would be lost.

Aurora blew her nose and spoke through her sobs. "Something awful . . . has happened to Harrison . . . I'm sure of it!"

Charlotte struggled to keep her own fears in check, forcing out words that hid her doubts. "Dear Lord, help Nat and Seth to find Harrison, and bring all three of them back safely. Amen."

Aurora's arms came about Charlotte, clinging to her while she cried even harder. "Harrison's been hurt . . . or drowned . . . I just know it!"

Charlotte held Aurora, feeling the dampness of her tears against her own face. She thought of Seth. What if he were to drown?

A searing pain cut through her stomach, sending agonizing jolts throughout her body. She couldn't bear to lose Seth now, not after all they'd been through, not after they'd come this far!

She squeezed her eyes shut. Seth was there, his lopsided grin revealing the crooked front tooth. There was a self-assurance about him, an air of invincibility. His image infused her with confidence.

Several moments later, when Aurora's weeping had subsided, Charlotte said in a half whisper, "You can count on Seth. He'll take care of Harrison."

Gradually, Aurora's crying abated and she released

Charlotte, dabbing away tears with an already-soaked handkerchief. Charlotte pulled her own from her pocket and offered it to her.

Aurora blew her nose, then looked directly into Charlotte's eyes with her swollen ones. "Do you really think Harrison will be all right?"

She thought of the man her sister was to marry. For years, he had been as dependable as a rock in his position as second assistant keeper on South Manitou, and in his wooing of Aurora. His reliability had earned him the assistant keeper's position at the new light on North Manitou. If anyone knew the Manitous, the perils of the passage, and how to weather them, surely it was Harrison. Her eyes steady on Aurora's, she answered, "I'm sure of it."

At that, Aurora's mouth turned upward ever so slightly at the corner. "Thank you, Charlotte. I needed to hear you say that." She got up and lit the lantern by the bed. It cast a soft glow on the tray on the night stand. She lifted the upturned plate that covered her dinner and bent to take in the aroma. "Maybe I am a little hungry," she admitted. "Would you sit with me while I eat?"

It was nearly seven by the time Charlotte took Aurora's half-empty tray back downstairs. As she passed the front room, she saw that at least a dozen of the islanders had gathered there. Mrs. Garrity and Nat's father-in-law, Otto Schroeder, were among them. Mr. Trevelyn was there, too, still in his heavy jacket, evidently just in from adjusting the lamp in the tower. More snow-dusted guests were coming in through the side entrance. Bridget and Mrs. Trevelyn were pouring coffee for neighbors who spoke in hushed tones as if in a funeral parlor. The adjacent dining room, which had been arranged temporarily as a second sitting room, held an overflow of worried friends, and a table piled high with wedding gifts.

In the basement kitchen, a platter of tiny sandwiches had been artfully arranged and set on the baker's cabinet. Charlotte's mother was measuring more coffee into the pot, and paused to glance Charlotte's way as she scraped Aurora's leftovers into the scrap bucket. "I'm glad to see the girl has eaten something. She's as tiny as I am plump. I worry about her when her appetite is off." She set the pot on the burner, unlatched the stove door with a hot pad, and bent to toss in two more pieces of hardwood, swinging the door shut with a clank. "How many guests do we have upstairs, now?"

Charlotte thought a moment. "About twenty, I would guess."

Julia clucked her tongue. "You'd better go up with that platter of sandwiches. I'll bring more coffee as soon as it's ready. It looks like we have a long night ahead of us."

Charlotte passed the sandwiches to the guests, found space for the half-empty platter on the table beside the untouched wedding cake in the front room, then joined Mrs. Garrity, Otto Schroeder, and Mr. Trevelyn.

"Dis est ugly weather," Otto bemoaned in his thick accent. "Ven Seth come und fetch Nat, I send Fritz mit dem. 'Fritz,' I say, 'mit doze strong arms, you can keep one hot fire in dat boiler. Den Seth can help his bruder up on deck.'"

"That was good of you, Otto," said Mr. Trevelyn to his longtime friend. "Fritz certainly has a set of muscles from working those draft horses in your fields. I know my boys can use an extra crewman on a night like this."

"Maybe they've found Harrison and Preacher Mulder by now," conjectured Mrs. Garrity. "On the other hand, I can't help wondering if they turned around and went back to Glen Arbor after the wind came up."

Though Charlotte's intuition told her otherwise, she tested her teacher's line of thinking. "They might have had second thoughts once they left the protection of Sleeping Bear Bay," she reasoned. "The passage would have presented much heavier winds, and rougher seas."

Seth's father shook his head. "I know Harrison. He's a man of his word. He'd do everything he could to get here. It's a matter of honor with him. Besides, he would have been too far from the mainland to turn back by the time the wind whipped up." Mr. Trevelyn checked his timepiece. "Now, if you'll excuse me, I'd better see to my light."

On the port deck near the bow of the *Manitou Lady*, Seth's fleece-lined leather cap shielded him from the worst of the cold air. Fortunately, the wind was dying down, and he could keep his back to the occasional stiff gust while he attempted to see past the deck lamps for some sign of Harrison's sloop. He clung to the rail, steadying himself against the pitch of the boat as it rode the six-foot waves, thankful that a clearing line had moved across the passage, pushing clouds and snow out of the way to reveal a three-quarters moon that lit the water's surface.

Five hours had passed since he had left the keeper's quarters. He was thankful for Fritz Schroeder's willingness to tend the furnace. Plenty of time had been spent getting to the boat, taking on fuel, and firing up the boiler, a process that would have taken longer without the help of Nat's brawny brother-in-law.

At first, they had headed in the direction of Glen Arbor, but conditions quickly told them that Harrison's sloop would have been forced toward North Manitou, so they had turned toward the island, zig zagging in an effort to find him. How he wished with the crest of each wave that the bridegroom's boat would come in sight.

In the far distance he could see the blinking red and white light on the North Manitou tower. By his judgment, they were not far from the dangerous rocky shoals at the southwest corner of the island. He feared that Harrison's boat could have broken up on the rocks, and that the same fate could befall the *Manitou Lady* if Nat steered too close.

Seth pulled his scarf more tightly about his neck and face and closed his eyes for a moment. Charlie's image came to him, safe and warm by the sitting room fire. How he longed to be with her. Not just for his own comfort and safety, but because he thought about her constantly whenever they were apart.

He opened his eyes and blinked, then blinked again. Could that be a boat off the port side of the *Manitou Lady*? He steadied his gaze while the next wave crested.

There it was! The hull of a boat! But there was no mast, and he could make out only one person aboard.

Seth shouted to his brother in the pilothouse. "There's a boat off the port side!"

"Harrison's?"

"I can't tell until we're closer. Turn to port." Seth hurried to the deck below. He could hear faint cries for help, barely audible above the noise of the steamer.

Nat's maneuvering brought them close enough for Seth to recognize Harrison's sailboat, but its mast was broken. Within moments, they were close enough for Seth to see that Preacher Mulder was trying to row against the waves, dragging the heavy, wet canvas sail that floated on the surface. But why was Harrison lying on the bottom of the boat, his back propped against the bow?

With no time for questions, Seth grabbed the *Manitou Lady's* line and tied three heavy knots in the end of it.

"I'll toss a rope," he shouted to the reverend. "Tie it tight. We'll pull you alongside and take you aboard." He swung and tossed. The line hit inside the bow, then slipped over the gunwale into the water.

Seth reeled it in, swung it about his head, and tossed again.

This time, the rope landed almost in Preacher Mulder's lap, but before he could get a secure grip on it, a swell lifted the sailboat, and it slipped through his hands.

Nat stuck his head out of the pilothouse. "Seth! Get below and give me full steam astern! We're almost on the rocks!"

With all the strength he could summon, Seth tossed the line again. Again, it landed in the preacher's lap.

Not waiting to see whether he was able to tie it off securely, Seth dashed below, set the engine controls full astern, then joined Fritz at the furnace.

"Stoke the fire! We're nearly on the shoals!" he shouted above the throbbing of the engine.

Fritz pitched in the last of the coal while Seth attacked the wood supply, enraging the orange flames in the fire box.

By ten o'clock, despite improvements in the weather that raised the temperature above freezing, decreased the wind to a whisper, and quieted the rolling waves to medium-sized lazy swells, a pall of gloom had fallen over the wedding guests. As Charlotte passed a replenished tray of sandwiches, few words were spoken by the two dozen or so islanders who seemed to have settled in until news of the missing bridegroom and preacher and their search party had arrived.

When she had circulated through the sitting rooms, Charlotte returned to the front parlor to leave the remaining sandwiches on the table beside the wedding cake. She paused a moment to reflect on the three-tiered confection that still stood intact, monument to the ceremony that never was. Beside it, the perfectly arranged plates, forks, and napkins remained untouched as well. The same couldn't be said for the punch bowl, which now held only a small puddle at the very bottom.

She was trying to decide whether to go down to the kitchen to help her mother, or to check on Aurora upstairs, when she heard the rustle of satin. In the doorway stood her sister in her wedding gown, a fragile smile on her pretty mouth as she stepped into the room to face her guests. A murmur could be heard rippling through the back sitting room until its connecting doorway was filled with the faces of curious guests.

Silence fell. Everyone seemed to be holding their breath. Aurora scanned the room, then cleared her throat.

"I came—"

Charlotte stood closest to her sister, yet she could barely hear the thin voice. A hush moved through those gathered as guests at the back asked the ones at the front what the bride had said.

Aurora started again. "I came downstairs to thank you all for coming," she said with surprising volume and clarity. "And . . . because I'm hungry." She turned around, picked up the beribboned cake knife, sliced herself a respectable piece of wedding cake, and slid it onto a plate. Taking up a fork and napkin, she faced her guests again. "Please help yourselves. No point in letting it go to waste." Eyes glistening with unshed tears, she added, "Now, if you'll excuse me—" With grace and elegance, she exited the room, her train flowing behind.

As Charlotte went to carry Aurora's train up the stairs, she heard sympathetic murmurs. "Heartbroken . . . Poor little thing . . . Brave, isn't she?"

In her bedroom once again, Aurora turned tearfully to Charlotte and handed her the cake. "You eat it," She said shakily, brushing a tear from her cheek with the back of her hand. Then her face crumpled, and she began to sob openly. "Oh Charlotte . . . I don't know what I'll do without Harrison!"

Charlotte set the cake on her dresser and put her arms about Aurora. "There, now," she comforted, determined to hide her own fears. "Don't go thinking the worst. Not until—"

Until what? Until Nat and Seth came home with bad news? What if they didn't return, either? A chill passed through her at the thought that with the light of day could come the most devastating news ever to hit the island.

Charlotte bit her lip. *I will not give in to such thinking,* she silently chided herself. With new resolve, she released herself from Aurora. "It's just a matter of time before Harrison comes to claim you as his bride. I'm sure of it. Now, I'm going up to the watch room. The moment I see something, I'll let you know."

CHAPTER 22

Charlotte pulled on her coat and headed through the passage and up the stairs for the first time in hours. With the number of guests at the keeper's quarters, and Aurora indisposed, her time had been divided between helping her mother in the kitchen, assisting Bridget and Mrs. Trevelyn with the serving, and ministering to the unwed bride.

Mr. Trevelyn was already in the watch room, studying the night waters through binoculars. He handed her the glasses.

"See if you find anything near the southwest end of North Manitou."

Charlotte adjusted the focus on the blinking red and white light that had gone into operation only two months earlier on North Manitou, and scanned the area just short of it. "Not a thing," she admitted reluctantly. "Why?"

"For a while, I saw a light moving back and forth, as if a boat was searching the water this side of the island. Then it moved south and eventually disappeared. If it was the *Manitou Lady*, either the boys found what they were looking for, or—

"Don't say it, Mr. Trevelyn," Charlotte cautioned, her voice full of dread. They both knew of the wide shoal area stretching into the passage from North Manitou.

"I don't think it was the *Manitou Lady*, after all," Seth's father said. "Seems to me it would have turned back this way if it were the boys. I'm going in to warm up."

As Charlotte continued searching the area between the two islands, her thoughts seemed to take a turn as dark as the water that flowed beyond the tower's beam. Despite the fact that both Nat and Seth were well-acquainted with the shoal waters, the *Manitou Lady* could have strayed off course. A chill washed over her, bringing with it the dread and fear she had felt the last time she had been in the tower.

If the boat hit rocks, within moments Nat, Seth and Fritz would be fighting for their lives in water barely above freezing. Even if they managed to hang onto life rings or a piece of wreckage, within a short time they would be too numb to help themselves.

Tears clouded her vision. She set down the binoculars, disappointed with herself for letting her fears get out of control, but her thoughts raced on. *I hate this island. I hate it! It's taken from me the two men I have loved most! If Seth dies, I'll go away and never set foot here again!*

Weeping uncontrollably, she buried her face in her hands. If Seth were no longer a part of her future, she had little to look forward to. The past several days had been her happiest ever, knowing they would go through life together. A future without Seth was like a future without sunshine and joy.

Several minutes later, she managed to staunch the flow of her tears. Though bereft of all hope, she glanced out the watch room window one last time. Something so strange caught her attention that she closed her eyes, then looked again.

The light on North Manitou was blinking, but not in its red-white pattern. Only the white light flashed, and not in its steady ten-second rhythm.

She caught her breath and watched. Blink, blink, blink. Then a pause. Then three more white flashes with irregular timing.

Charlotte patted her cheeks to make certain she wasn't dreaming and looked again. The white light flashed slowly three times, then after a few seconds of darkness, showed a series of flashes—long-short-long.

Her heart almost stopped, then tears began streaming down her face—tears of happiness this time—until she could hardly see anything at all! She blinked the water from her eyes, wiping her cheeks with her hands, watching the signal again and again.

Seth was alive! He would be coming home! She wanted to shout the news from the top of the tower!

Instead, she kept watching the blessed pattern, until finally, after several minutes, the steady red and white ten-second rhythm of the North Manitou light reappeared.

As fast as her feet could carry her, Charlotte dashed down the tower stairs, through the keeper's quarters, and up to the bedroom to tell Aurora the news.

On the deck of the *Manitou Lady*, Helen Garrity pulled her warm winter coat more snugly about the green silk spring ensemble George had brought her two and a half years ago, and turned her face to the sunshine, a rare treat for the last week of November. So what if her toilet was not in keeping with the season!

At last, she had managed to gain a much-needed perspective on her life, thanks to Charlie Richards. Actually, the young woman had no idea how much she had helped her former teacher. Her return to South Manitou had presented the perfect solution to finding a competent, caring teacher who could take over in the one-room school—someone who loved both the children and the island dearly. And come spring, the new bride and groom would move into her cabin to set up housekeeping.

Helen also had Charlie to thank for giving her the courage to actively pursue her own happiness, rather than simply waiting for life's joy to come her way. The young woman had been brave enough to venture to the mainland to seek her future, and wise enough to know that for her, it lay on the island.

Helen had been distraught enough to seek refuge on the same island, and only now, courageous enough to admit that her happiness lay on the mainland.

Thank goodness for the *Manitou Lady* needing winter repairs in Frankfort, and her owners being gracious enough to take a teacher there with them. Within hours, she would be bound for Detroit by train.

She wondered what George would think when he saw her. The thought was a little unnerving, but that couldn't change the fact that deep within her, she now felt a brightness she hadn't known in years, a contentment that would grow with each passing day, and a confidence that when she was with George once again, they would get along very nicely together!

ABOUT DONNA WINTERS

Donna adopted Michigan as her home state in 1971 when she moved there from a small town outside of Rochester, New York. She began penning novels in 1982 while working full time for Lear/Siegler, Inc. (now Smiths Industries), of Grand Rapids.

She resigned in 1984 following a contract offer for her first book. Since then, she has written six romance novels for various publishers, including Thomas Nelson Publishers and Zondervan Publishing House.

Her husband, Fred, an American History teacher, shares her enthusiasm for history. Together, they visit historical sites, restored villages, museums, and lake ports, purchasing books and reference materials for use in Donna's research and Fred's classroom. One recent excursion took her to several lighthouses of the Great Lakes, including the South Manitou Island light, Raspberry Island light in the Apostle Islands, and the lights at Two Harbors and Split Rock in Minnesota.

Donna has lived all of her life in states bordering on the Great Lakes. Her familiarity and fascination with these remarkable inland waters and her residence in the heart of Great Lakes Country make her the perfect candidate for writing *Great Lakes Romances*®. (Photo by Renee Werni.)

ABOUT THE ARTIST

Patrick Kelley has always liked to draw. Nurturing his dream of one day seeing his work in print, he attended art school in his hometown of Grand Rapids, Michigan, completing his Bachelor of Fine Arts Degree at Kendall College of Art and Design in 1987.

A freelance artist since 1985, his creative ability has served clients such as American Greetings and Butterworth Hospital. Several of his illustrations have been published, appearing in the Michigan Sports Gazette, Grand Rapids Magazine, and West Michigan Magazine.

Mr. Kelley's proficient use of airbrush, colored pencils, and stabilo pencils, along with his excellent draftsmanship and innate ability to interpret rough concepts into engaging designs, make him popular with his clients, and a winner at art shows. Over the years, he has earned first place awards for his work in pastels, photography, and watercolor.

Bigwater Publishing is pleased to feature the work of this talented Michigan artist on the cover of *Charlotte of South Manitou Island*.

MORE GREAT LAKES ROMANCES

MACKINAC
by Donna Winters
First in the series of *Great Lakes Romances*
(Set on Mackinac Island, 1895.)

Her name bespoke the age in which she lived . . .

But **Victoria Whitmore** was no shy, retiring Victorian miss. Never a homebody, attending to the whims of her cabinetmaker Papa, she found herself aboard the *Algomah*, traveling from staid Grand Rapids to Michigan's fashionable Mackinac Island resort.

Her journey was not one of pleasure; a restful holiday did not await her. Mackinac's Grand Hotel owed the Whitmores money—enough to save the furniture manufactory from certain financial ruin. It became Victoria's mission to venture to the island to collect the payment. At Mackinac, however, her task was anything but easy, and she found more than she had bargained for.

Rand Bartlett, the hotel manager, was part of that bargain. Accustomed to challenges and bent on making the struggling Grand a success, he had not counted on the challenge of Victoria—and he certainly had not counted on losing his heart to her.

The Captain and the Widow
by Donna Winters
Second in the series of *Great Lakes Romances*
(Set in Chicago, South Haven, and Mackinac Island, 1897.)

Lily Atwood Haynes is beautiful, intelligent, and ahead of her time . . .

But even her grit and determination have not prepared her for the cruel event on Lake Michigan that leaves her widowed at age twenty. It is the lake—with its fathomless depths and unpredictable forces—that has provided her livelihood. Now it is the lake that challenges her newfound happiness.

When **Captain Hoyt Curtiss**, her husband's best friend, steps in to

offer assistance in navigating the choppy waters of Lily's widowhood, she can only guess at the dark secret that shrouds his past and chokes his speech. What kind of miracle will it take to forge a new beginning for *The Captain and the Widow?*
Note: The Captain and the Widow *is a spin-off from* Mackinac.

Sweethearts of Sleeping Bear Bay
by Donna Winters
Third in the series of *Great Lakes Romances*
(Set in the Sleeping Bear Dune region of
northern Michigan, 1898.)

Mary Ellen Jenkins is a woman of rare courage and experience . . .
One of only four females licensed as navigators and steamboat masters on the Western Rivers, she is accustomed to finding her way through dense fog on the Mississippi. But when she travels North for the first time in her twenty-nine years, she discovers herself unprepared for the havoc caused by a vaporous shroud off ***Sleeping Bear Point***. And navigating the misty shoals of her own uncertain future poses an even greater threat to her peace of mind.

Self-confident, skilled, and devoted to his duties as Second Mate aboard the Lake Michigan sidewheeler, *Lily Belle*, **Thad Grant** regrets his promise to play escort to the petticoat navigator the instant he lays eyes on her plain face. Then his career runs aground. Can he trust this woman to guide him to safe harbor, or will the Lady Reb ever be able to overcome the great gulf between them?
Note: Sweethearts of Sleeping Bear Bay *is a spin-off from* The Captain and the Widow.

Jenny of L'Anse Bay
by Donna Winters
Special Edition in the series of *Great Lakes Romances*
(Set in the Keweenaw Peninsula in 1867.)

A raging fire destroys more than Jennifer Crawford's new home; it also burns a black hole into her future. To soothe Jennifer's resentful spirit, her parents send her on a trip with their pastor and his wife to the Indian mission at L'Anse Bay. In the wilderness of Michigan's Upper Peninsula, Jennifer soon moves from tourist to teacher, taking over the education of the Ojibway children. Without knowing their language, she must teach them English, learn their customs, and live in harmony with them.

Hawk, son of the Ojibway chief, teaches Jennifer the ways of his tribe. Often discouraged by seemingly insurmountable cultural barriers, Jennifer must also battle danger, death, and the fears that threaten to come between her and the man she loves.

Sweet Clover: A Romance of the White City
Centennial Edition in the series of *Great Lakes Romances*
(Set in Chicago at the World's Columbian Exposition of 1893.)

THE WORLD'S COLUMBIAN EXPOSITION of 1893 brought unmatched excitement and wonder to Chicago, thus inspiring Clara Louise Burnham's novel, *Sweet Clover: A Romance of the White City*, first published in 1894.

A Chicago resident from age nine, Burnham penned her novels in an apartment overlooking Lake Michigan. Her romance books contain innocent tales imbued with the customs and morals of a bygone era—stories that garnered a sizable loyal readership in their day.

In Clara Louise Burnham's novel, *Sweet Clover*, a destitute heroine of twenty enters a marriage of convenience to ensure the security and well-being of her fatherless family. Widowed soon after, Clover Bryant Van Tassel strives to rebuild a lifelong friendship with her late husband's son. Jack Van Tassel had been her childhood playmate, and might well have become her suitor. Believing himself betrayed by both his father and the girl he once admired, the Chicagoan moves far away from his native city. Then the World's Columbian Exposition opens, luring Jack once again to his old family home.

Hearts warmed by friendship blossom with affection—in some most surprising ways. Will true love come to all who seek it in the Fair's fabulous White City? The author will keep you guessing till the very end!

ORDER FORM

Customer Name ______________________________

Address ______________________________

____

____

Available while supplies last.

Quantity		Total
	75-8. *Mackinac*, \$6.95	
	76-6. *The Captain and the Widow*, \$6.95	
	77-4. *Sweethearts of Sleeping Bear Bay*, \$7.95	
	79-0. *Charlotte of South Manitou Island*, \$8.95	
	78-2. *Jenny of L'Anse Bay*, \$7.95	
	80-4. *Sweet Clover: A Romance of the White City*, \$8.95	
	Subtotal:	
	Michigan residents include 4% tax:	
	Postage-add \$1.05 for first item, 50¢ for each additional (maximum - \$3):	
	Total:	

Send check or money order to:
Bigwater Publishing
P.O. Box 177
Caledonia, MI 49316